PENGUIN BOOKS

THE URGE TO DIE

Peter Giovacchini, M.D., is a psychoanalyst and
Clinical Professor of Psychiatry at the University
of Illinois in Chicago. He is nationally known for
his work with adolescents and their problems.

THE
URGE
TO DIE

PETER GIOVACCHINI, M.D.

PENGUIN
BOOKS

Penguin Books Ltd, Harmondsworth,
Middlesex, England
Penguin Books, 625 Madison Avenue,
New York, New York 10022, U.S.A.
Penguin Books Australia Ltd, Ringwood,
Victoria, Australia
Penguin Books Canada Limited, 2801 John Street,
Markham, Ontario, Canada L3R 1B4
Penguin Books (N.Z.) Ltd, 182–190 Wairau Road,
Auckland 10, New Zealand

First published in the United States of America
with the subtitle *Why Young People Commit Suicide* by
Macmillan Publishing Co., Inc., 1981
Published in Penguin Books 1983

LIBRARY OF CONGRESS CATALOGING IN PUBLICATION DATA
Giovacchini, Peter L.
    The urge to die.
    Bibliography: p.
    1. Youth—United States—Suicidal behavior.
2. Suicide—United States—Prevention. 3. Adolescence.
4. Adolescent psychology. I. Title.
HV6546.G56 1983   616.85'8445   82-16550
ISBN 0 14 00.6314 5

Printed in the United States of America by
R. R. Donnelley & Sons Company, Harrisonburg, Virginia
Set in Baskerville

ACKNOWLEDGMENTS

I WISH TO EXPRESS my appreciation to Toni Lopopolo, who recognized the importance of a book on this subject, and to Bruce Michael Gans for his indispensable editorial assistance in the preparation of the manuscript.

NOTE TO THE READER

WITH THE EXCEPTION of the first example of an adolescent suicide, which was reported in the public media, all other clinical examples have been sufficiently disguised to protect the privacy of the persons involved.

Contents

APPENDICES

PART ONE

Why Should We Live?

There is but one truly philosophical problem, and that is
suicide. Judging whether life is or is not worth living
amounts to answering the fundamental question. . . . all
the rest . . . comes afterwards. . . . I see many people die
because they judge that life is not worth living. I see others
killed for ideas or illusions that give them a reason for
living (what is called a reason for living is also an excellent
reason for dying). I therefore conclude that the meaning of
life is the most urgent of questions. How to answer it?

ALBERT CAMUS

CHAPTER 1

An Introduction

JEFFREY HUNTER was an outgoing, athletic, seemingly happy adolescent who attended Ridgewood High School in Ridgewood, New Jersey. Toward the latter part of 1978, at the age of sixteen, Jeffrey hanged himself.

Hours after he was buried a number of his fellow students were sitting together trying to figure out why. Suddenly Christopher Mathieson, a moody loner, aged sixteen, leapt up and sped home mumbling that he had something to do. Shortly thereafter he was found, hanged, in a stairway closet.

These two boys were the third and fourth suicides at this high school within the past year and a half. In reporting the incident *Time* magazine said, "the deaths could have happened almost anywhere in the United States."

Like Jeffrey and Christopher, Laurie attended a top-notch, highly competitive high school located in an affluent suburb. The shy, petite seventeen-year-old came from a good home and had always done well academically. She had always been a very private girl, dating only occasionally. Her only confidante was Alice, a girl friend who moved to another state just before the start of Laurie's senior year. Laurie missed her friend keenly and wrote her on a weekly basis. Soon her friend's replies became more and more infrequent.

Laurie's grades began to plummet precipitously. She became withdrawn and lost her appetite, sometimes going two and three days with almost no food. When her parents asked her about this, or her future plans, Laurie averted her eyes, shrugged, and muttered, "What's the point?" or "Who cares?" Five weeks had gone by since Alice had failed to answer Laurie's last letter. Three days after Laurie was accepted to a Big Ten school she snatched her mother's car keys, stole out to the garage, and was found dead of carbon monoxide poisoning in the morning. As with most cases of adolescent suicide, Laurie's death did not appear in the newspapers.

George was a witty, personable, intellectually curious sixteen-year-old. However, that was not how George viewed himself. Although he dated as often as anyone else, he thought he was terribly unattractive and felt somehow that girls were doing him a favor by going out with him. Preoccupied and utterly bedeviled by such questions as Who am I? What is the meaning of life? What can I do well? he thought surely he was the most insecure and miserable student in his class. The one flair he did have, as far as he was concerned, was journalism, and he threw himself into the high school newspaper activities with all his being. But he also desperately craved to be popular and toward the end of the spring semester he ran for senior class president. On a Monday he received an F on a page-makeup assignment, which caused him to become deeply troubled. The following day he came in a very distant second in the class election. Somehow, in his mind, George had always thought suicide a romantic notion, something that sensitive, tormented natures turn to. That evening, while his parents were watching television in the living room, he locked himself in the bathroom and swallowed twenty-five sleeping tablets. His parents discovered him and rushed him to the hospital. After a three-day stay, no permanent damage was discovered and he was released. He returned to school and started to see a therapist, something his parents had previously forbidden since they felt that George, like everybody else, had to learn to handle his own problems alone.

The above stories concern the subject of this book: suicide among adolescents. The stories have been presented in a somewhat dramatic fashion, which, in a sense, mirrors the dramatic dimensions the problem has assumed within the recent past. Years ago, adolescent suicide was a relatively rare and isolated phenomenon. When it did occur, it was generally hushed up. Those who had attempted and failed were considered skeletons in the family closet.

Today the problem of adolescent suicide is only beginning to be openly acknowledged and discussed. On the basis of statistics alone it deserves our pressing attention.

Nationally, youthful suicides have tripled over the last two decades. Between 1950 and 1960 they had doubled. Sources indicate that about 10,000 people between the ages of fifteen and thirty-four take their own lives every year. The adolescent suicide rate is nearly 33 percent higher than that of the overall population. It is the third leading cause of adolescent death, following homicide and accidents. Even here the actual numbers of suicides may be larger than suspected. For among those who die by accident there are undoubtedly some who have had a history of relating to the world in a self-defeating and reckless manner.

They often place themselves in dangerous situations by driving carelessly, pulling stunts with motorcycles, or experimenting with dangerous drugs.

Their deaths often seem accidental; perhaps they are. Any objective observer, however, would see clearly that this particular group, within the larger number of accident fatalities, were deceiving themselves. By resisting the efforts of adults who try to help them they continue on the path of self-destruction.

They are just as intent on killing themselves as those who do so in a more overt way. In short, it is estimated that, although attempted suicides often go unreported or disguised in hospital reports, perhaps as many as a quarter of a million adolescents make a serious unsuccessful effort to kill themselves every year.

In the past, the suicide rate among the poor and minority groups was higher than that of the affluent white population. Today the two are little more than a percentage point apart, the highest recorded rates of the century and the lowest white-nonwhite ratio ever.

In brief, adolescent suicide is an ever growing, ever more disturbing dilemma that now encompasses every economic and social stratum in contemporary America.

Obviously the situation raises a host of fundamental questions. Why do adolescents commit and attempt suicide in such comparatively large numbers? Why is the incidence rising? What are the successful and the attempted suicides trying to tell us? What are they asking for? Why is adolescence such a vulnerable, often precarious stage of human development in our civilization? Anyone who has been deeply involved with adolescents knows what a difficult, baffling, and often frustrating group they are to deal with effectively. How can a concerned parent or high school teacher reach a better understanding of adolescence and thereby help teenagers arrive at the shores of adulthood strong and whole and eager for the life ahead of them?

These are the questions, among others, that *The Urge to Die* intends to address. The approach, the scope, the substance, and the limitations of our inquiry are all based upon my work as a psychoanalyst who has done a great deal of work centered on adolescents.

One overriding lesson my practice has consistently taught me is that people, their needs, their conflicts, their instincts, their environment are all infinitely complex, far more complex than any computer or mathematical equation. It would be misleading, as well as a disservice to the nature and the magnitude of teenage suicide, to suggest that there are any absolute answers, a set of simple, easy equations that, once learned, will automatically and completely eradicate the problem.

The reasons adolescents take their own lives have their roots in the strengths and the deficits incorporated during earliest childhood, in the nature of the society and the family in which they currently live, and in the conflicts and traumas they encounter in everyday life. In each case the person's motivations, as well as the interplay of the previously mentioned factors, differ.

This is not to say that much cannot be done to rectify the dilemma. Sigmund Freud, the founder of modern psychoanalysis, theorized toward the end of his clinical career that a death instinct inhabits the soul of humans and animals alike. Subsequent research has found no evidence to support that contention. By all accounts, teenagers, like the rest of us, have an innate urge to live and prosper. Psychoanalysis has always been unreservedly on the side of living. It operates under the assumption that human beings can be helped significantly to lead successful, gratifying lives.

Rather than dealing in simple formulas, the field of psychiatry has done effective work through an understanding of what adolescence is as a biological, emotional, and social stage of human development. It has evolved a set of general principles that permit its practitioners to recognize and resolve self-destructive impulses.

Generally speaking, this is what *The Urge to Die* hopes to convey. The framework it presents will draw upon lessons and principles from psychiatric practice and research. It will also draw upon sociological findings and illustrate the difficulties teenagers encounter by presenting a variety of representative profiles of troubled adolescents.

By understanding what adolescence is, what it is attempting to accomplish, the nature of the stumbling blocks facing this age group, as well as some of the symptoms of the deeply troubled, the concerned layman should, at the very least, walk away with a fundamental grasp of the dilemma and a greater sensitivity to its nuances. *The Urge to Die* is especially intended for those who are most immediately immersed in the daily lives of teenagers: parents, guidance counselors, and other concerned adults. For it is this group who is invariably confronted, baffled, and devastated by the tragedy of self-inflicted deaths. They are also invariably the ones who have such a tremendous impact, for good or for inadvertent ill, on young people.

I happen to empathize deeply with both parts (I refuse to say sides) of the teenage-adult relationship. Adults viewing and attempting to guide teenagers have a difficult time seeing them so completely confused and distressed. Many members of the older generation spent their own adolescence in strapped economic circumstances. Today, in many cases, they find themselves confronted by the onset of health problems inevitable in the aging process. How difficult it must be to see teenagers who seem to lack nothing feel miserable. Most have had their material wants satisfied from birth. They now enjoy the near peak of their strength, good looks, and health. Not yet burdened by the need to earn a living, adolescents should be enjoying life.

Many of today's adolescents obviously do lack something. A fundamental principle of psychoanalysis is that every symptom, every conflict has an origin, a cause. A parent or teacher can hardly be condemned outright for failing to grasp how teenagers can be so troubled when "they've been given all the advantages we never had."

The French philosopher Jean-Paul Sartre, whom some consider the founder of existentialism, has expressed an equivalent attitude: "the exploitation of men by other men, undernourishment—these make *metaphysical unhappiness a*

luxury and relegate it to second place. Hunger—now that is
an evil." (Italics added.)

Allen Wheelis refutes Sartre, in the name of us all. His
reply is especially useful in beginning to recognize, appreciate, and ultimately cope with teenage suicide. He writes in
his novel *The Desert:*

> Many of us have never known this kind of misery, have never
> felt a lash or club, never been shot at, persecuted, bombed, starved
> —yet we suffer too. . . . We eat, often exceedingly well; the roof over
> our heads is timber and tile; we know deep carpets, thin china,
> great music, rare wine; a woman looks at us with love; we have
> friends, families, our needs are met. . . . Poets tell the truth. . . . It's
> part of being human, we differ from one another only in more or
> less. A few tranquil ones, with little conflict, suffer less; at the other
> extreme stretched by despair to some dreadful cracking point, one
> goes berserk. In between are the rest of us, not miserable enough
> to go mad or jump off the bridge, yet never able if we are honest
> to say that we have come to terms with life, are at peace with our-
> selves, that we are happy. . . . Wealth and intelligence and good
> fortune are no protection. Having good parents helps but guaran-
> tees nothing; misery comes with the gold spoon, to the prince and
> princess and the ladies-in-waiting, to groom and gamekeeper, to the
> mighty and the humble.
> We feel our suffering as alien, desperately unwanted, yet nothing
> imposes it.

Adolescence itself is a particularly precarious, comparatively short transitional period in which a child is expected
to be transformed into an adult. By definition it must be
a period of constant change. Change, by its nature, means
instability. Adolescence is also a state of becoming, a period
in which each person forges, however imperfectly, the self-
esteem, the sense of individuality, the values, and the coping
skills that he or she must depend upon in adulthood. It is
an enormous task even in the most supportive and stable
environments. It is not accomplished in a formal, rational,
structured fashion, but rather piecemeal, instinctively, unconsciously. In our society, in which everything from cultural mores down to the cohesiveness of the basic family

unit is often riddled by instability, it is little wonder why an adolescent's struggle can sometimes end disastrously.

One of the most tragic aspects of adolescent suicide, ironically enough, is also a source of great hope. I refer to the fact that many, if not all, of those teenagers who move to abort their lives could be saved. Tragedy and hope, in fact, will be a recurrent theme in our discussions. In the instance of adolescent suicide, they are really two sides of the same coin.

There are a number of reasons for this. For despite my professional and personal bias in favor of life, one must pose the question, Do not teenagers, like everyone else, have the right to choose whether to live? They are the ones who must live their lives. Therefore, are they not entitled to dispose of it as they see fit? Are there perfectly legitimate criteria by which one can dispassionately decide to die?

The tragedy, of course, is that real people in real life do not make such decisions. Studies have shown that the vast majority of those who have attempted to kill themselves were highly ambivalent about the act. In many of their minds they did not see themselves as departed at all but rather hovering invisibly over the ensuing scene, soothed or perhaps gloating over the grief of those whom they imagine mourning them. In short, they did not want to die. Their attempt to end their lives was a call for relief or help.

From our point of view the reasons that cause a teenager to end his or her life are by no means ironclad or irrefutable. In some cases a teenager may be driven by a "precipitating event," a rejection by a lover or a tongue lashing by a particularly critical parent. Without minimizing for a moment the anguish and the intensity of the conflict involved, it is fair to say that such teenagers have not developed the adaptive skills or the experience an adult might employ.

About thirty years ago a young man named Ross Lockridge took his life shortly after his first novel, *Raintree County*, became an enormous success. After his book's publication he became unaccountably depressed and listless. He felt consciously haunted by the conviction that he had nothing more to say and could never write again. A biographer theorized convincingly that the roots of Lockridge's depression and creative impotence were in unconscious conflicts. Without realizing it, Lockridge had been motivated to excel by a desire to impress and please his mother while competing with his father. These are fundamental, virtually universal, human impulses which arise in childhood and which, when properly resolved, serve a positive utilitarian function in adult personalities. Somewhere in Lockridge's tormented psyche he was overwhelmed by vague guilt when his book made him far more successful than his father. On a primitive level he felt he had destroyed his father. Had he received effective psychiatric care, these and other hidden motives and impulses would probably have surfaced. His conscious mind would have recognized, and gone beyond, the fatal childlike forces within him.

The point is that many teenagers "driven" to suicide, driven to tragedy, can, with the appropriate intervention, be redirected to hope. A good percentage of those who are rescued go on to lead productive lives. In my view, and it is by no means unique, the urge to die, especially in teenagers, is really in essence an urge to live that has somehow been derailed. No one who has been involved with adolescents needs to be convinced of the enormous fund of sheer energy and enthusiasm they possess. Helping to rechannel and unleash that vibrant positive life force is one of the most gratifying experiences both an analyst and a layman can have.

To make a useful, though somewhat prosaic analogy, it is difficult for anyone who has learned to swim to identify, on an immediate and visceral level, with someone who stands before the shore, desperately wanting to acquire the skill, and even more desperately afraid of the water. The ability to identify, however, gives a teacher enormous insights into the difficulties a student is struggling to overcome. This type of understanding can be extremely helpful to the teenager and sustain him through the difficult developmental tasks that characterize adolescence.

Without suggesting that *The Urge to Die* provides ultimate panaceas (a concept, incidentally, that people need during adolescence and subsequently go beyond), I have incorporated a series of practical measures that I believe can enable a concerned adult to isolate and maybe supply the missing links in a troubled teenager's environment.

One thing to keep in mind at the outset is that there is no such thing as the perfectly brought-up child. Perfection in child rearing, as in every other form of human activity, is something one can only aim at with the prior knowledge that a good approximation is about the best anybody can realistically hope for.

Another basic tenet is that one of the most important abilities an adult can cultivate is to be able to put oneself in a teenager's shoes. Being able to feel approximately what a teenager is going through while standing desperately before the water is an important step toward understanding and communicating.

Teenagers, whether they are suicidal or not, are invariably obsessed with the questions, What is the purpose of life? Why should I live and for what? They are very good questions, questions that have engaged the full energies of our greatest philosophers, poets, and novelists. When in touch with teenagers we are likely to reexamine the answers we supplied and then buried many years ago. We bring, presumably, far greater experience and judgment to the fundamental question. In questioning, along with them, our basic assumptions, we ourselves may be renewed and reinvigorated by the new ways of looking at the world we evolve. In helping them survive and grow, they prod us into a new level of growth.

Novelist Peter Taylor, in one of his stories, depicted the

dilemma of a young married academic who was about to conclude, with his young family, a year's stay in Paris. In the last scene, he is sitting alone nursing a feeling of despondency. He is nursing it because it was a mood he often felt and savored during his adolescence. For a few bitter moments he deeply resents that he did not come to Paris when he was younger and single, that somehow it is now too late for him to experience the city as it should be, and that he has been cheated. Then his little daughter comes up to him and the mood is lost. Taylor writes:

They [his family] would never allow him to have it for days and days at a time as he once did. He felt a great loss, except he didn't really feel it, he only thought of it, [for] he had already established steady habits of work. He had acknowledged claims that others had on him . . . and [now] there were ideas and truths and work and people that he loved even better than himself.

This transition from adolescence to adulthood is one of the main topics of this book. I will begin by discussing adolescence as a stage of human development.

CHAPTER 2

Origins of Adolescent Suicide

> How can one trace the birth of the first ideas and impressions in a child's mind? Perhaps when a child begins to talk or even before but only gazes at everything with that dumb intent look that seems blank to grownups, it already catches and perceives the meaning and the connections of the events of his life, but is not able to tell it to himself or others.
>
> IVAN GONCHAROV

THE FOCUS OF THIS BOOK is on the present. In order to understand the nature of the problems that contribute to the rising incidence of adolescent suicide one must first understand its common emotional origins. Broadly speaking, that is the purpose of this chapter. It is also roughly the first step an analyst takes toward successfully treating this group.

An analyst recognizes that the problem stems from many sources, biological, physical, emotional, social, and familial. They are all inseparable components of the problem. In the course of our discussion we will be examining them all in depth. The general principles that underlie our understanding of an adolescent's intrapsychic needs, behavior, conflicts, and limitations are the same principles, in slightly different form, that underlie our understanding of an adolescent in his current environment.

People bring varying amounts of strengths and vulnerabilities to the task of adolescence. By the same token society brings its own particular set of values that are involved in assimilating adolescents into adulthood. In other places and at other times, both parties met the challenge with high degrees of success, or at least accommodation. It has been done in the past and with some understanding we can effectively help the system to work in the future.

In the meantime, our concern is to understand the difficulties that have arisen in our modern era between the adolescent and the external world. First, we have to define adolescence. I hasten to add that the nature of adolescence, and in a societal sense its very existence, varies from culture to culture. To get to the root of why adolescents commit suicide in our culture at this time one must grasp how early vulnerabilities surface, bend, and break under the stresses of this unstable age.

For this we must understand how human beings develop emotionally from infancy as well as why adolescence, as a stage of growth, works as it does. As our discussion will show, the principles of early development constitute the basis upon which we can analyze the other pieces of the puzzle. It leads naturally toward a discussion of here-and-now problems. Through them we can evolve an overall set of working principles.

There is a fundamental principle about adolescence. It is a stage of life that requires a stable, supportive environment within and outside the home. Adolescents need this support as an anchor against which they can work out the enormous uncertainties they so often struggle with.

Too often an adult actively involved with an adolescent inadvertently fails to recognize the signs that serious difficulties from an adolescent's remote past are surfacing again. An adolescent, for example, may lose a girl friend and react by weeping uncontrollably at the dinner table, curling up in his room and becoming so consumed by his loss that he all but ceases to function for months. An adult may well lose patience with such a reaction and finally excoriate the child for immaturity and insist he grow up. Without real-

izing it, the depth of his feeling may spring from an earlier
period when he felt that his mother did not love him. The
difference between an infant whose heart is broken and an
adolescent, unfortunately, is that an adolescent has sufficient physical maturity to act out his grief in a destructive
way—such as suicide.

The parent who has a grasp of and an appreciation for
some basic psychological principles will be much better prepared, in this case, to recognize that his child is at the mercy
of a much larger emotional problem, over which he has no
control, and which can be constructively resolved through
therapeutic assistance. An adolescent cannot be realistically
expected to comprehend objectively what is going on inside
him. Is that not what we mean when we say *unconscious*
motives? That is where an informed adult is needed.

What follows, therefore, are some essential concepts that
in themselves should tell us a great deal about an adolescent's emotional needs. Since these principles echo throughout the other spheres of an adolescent's life, our mastery of
them will provide us some tools for giving us an overall
understanding of the problem.

For the most part we think of adolescence today as a
period that extends from the ages of twelve through twenty.
Biologically, childhood ends with the maturation of one's
sexual glands. From a strictly physical point of view, the
changes that occur during puberty—rapid physical growth,
deepening voice, the appearance of facial hair for boys, and
the growth of breasts, the rounding of hips, and menstrua-
tion for girls—mean adulthood.

During adolescence the mind itself undergoes changes that
enable it to take on, for the first time, new ways of thinking
about and dealing with the world. The change is comparable to the way an infant's nervous system and coordination
evolve. At birth, the central nervous system is incompletely
developed. It still has higher stages to reach. Similarly, the

adolescent's mind is not fully formed. It also has to reach higher stages of development to enable it to acquire the adaptations necessary to cope with the increasingly complicated adult world.

The problem is that an adolescent is emotionally unequipped, for all practical purposes, to function as an adult. He or she in many ways has the psychological mind-set of a child.

In some small way we can begin to grasp the enormous task facing an adolescent by remembering dreams all of us have had, dreams analysts call "anxiety dreams." This is the type of dream in which we find ourselves taking an examination, a calculus final, for example, and suddenly realizing that we never had any mathematical aptitude whatsoever. Furthermore, the closer we get to the examination room, the more terrified we become as we realize that we have never attended a single calculus class all semester.

In other words, we are heading into a world full of pressure, one in which we are going to be finally evaluated and tested. There is nothing in our background that has, as far as we know, prepared us with the skills to go into the unknown and emerge a success, a competent, qualified person.

An adolescent does not draw quite the total blank our dreamer might. The ways adolescents react to the challenges of becoming adults are often inadequate and destructive for quite understandable reasons. It is probably fair to say that a person brings a world view to adolescence that must, in some way, reflect his background. He has acquired some skills that will be useful in dealing with adult problems. Still, in general, the tasks that suddenly confront him are experienced as overwhelming. Throughout their entire past lives they have learned to comprehend and get along in the world as a child. That was their "job." They mastered it thoroughly, but during adolescence they have to "resign" and find another type of employment which seemingly has very little to do with their past experience.

The world according to a child involves some very special concepts. It normally means seeing one's parents, and adults generally, as big, powerful, omnipotent beings. This provides him with a feeling of safety and security. The world, as we all know, can be a very cruel and threatening place. In the beginning a child needs the protection of a parent to survive. To the vast majority of children at about the age of twelve that is still fundamentally the case.

As children grow, they learn to do more and more things for themselves (going to and from school, completing homework, setting the dinner table, and so on). They have an emotional legacy from their earliest years in which they realized they were small, much smaller than their parents, and relatively helpless. Furthermore, throughout their entire lives adults have done things for them. On some level children realize that is because they were incapable of doing the very things they will soon be expected to do for themselves as adults.

In short, they have acquired one set of skills to adapt and survive and now they must start virtually from scratch in evolving a completely new set.

Having never been adults, adolescents have very little concrete idea, or experience, of what the world will require of them and whether they can successfully make the mysterious transition to adulthood. They are faced with having to learn to earn a living, to leave the home they have known all their lives, to find love and security.

The job is so enormous that behavioral scientists have characterized the period in which a person is expected to re-create himself—from child to adult—as that in which one acquires *new psychic structures*. That means an adolescent has to come up with totally new definitions of who he or she is, what his or her talents are, what the world is, how it stands in relation to him or her, and how to get along with it. Finding an answer to a particular question is not enough. An adolescent is also faced with the enormous task of sorting these questions out into some cohesive, comprehensive, systematic order that will be durable or flexible enough to rely upon for the rest of his or her life.

It is not enough simply to be able to list the ingredients one needs to build a building and gather them all in one place. One must also transform them into a structure. That is a long, arduous process that requires years of work. A successful business executive, for example, is the end product of a young person who had to laboriously find out who he was, what he wanted to do, how he was going to approach it, and how his position was going to gratify him.

The pressures to evolve a unique functioning individuality are intense and, to say the least, invariably disruptive. Typically there are several underlying factors that add to the pressures.

Perhaps the first is the awakening of one's sexuality. For males, in fact, adolescence provides not a smooth, gradual introduction into sexuality but a sudden thrust into the zenith of their adult sexual drive. As a rule, an adolescent's body matures at a rate that far outstrips his emotional development. His body grows up and leaves him with a still childish mind, one that is riddled by uncertainties, one that usually has to catch up as best it can, slowly and painfully.

Sexual impulses invariably propel an adolescent forward into the very immediate world of crushes and unrequited love. Shutting out all sexual thoughts and impulses from one's conscious mind would sap all the psychic energy an adolescent needs to work out the problems that beset him.

In addition to budding sexuality there are other factors that can make an adolescent's life difficult. Adolescents want to be adults and want to find out who they are, but they do not have sophisticated adult techniques. What they typically fall back upon, unconsciously, are the roughly analogous experiences they had when very young and the way they handled them. These lessons are reactivated during adolescence.

Sharon's experiences as an entering high school sophomore serve as a good example. She was a popular girl who
had been elected to the student council that year. She was
obviously capable and bright and was soon appointed to
chair a subcommittee comprised largely of teenage boys.
Here was Sharon's first real opportunity at taking on adult
responsibilities, acting in an official capacity, and serving as
an administrator with some authority. Yet from virtually the
very first meeting she chaired, Sharon found herself anxious
and inhibited with her fellow members.

She had grown up with a father who had generally refused to concede that she or her mother was capable of
making choices and decisions that were as intelligent as his
own. Her father always had to have the last word, and
Sharon had witnessed this overbearing male assertiveness
since she was old enough to understand English.

When it came time for her to deal with young men in
an "adult" fashion she "instinctively" felt that they were all
out to get her, that they did not listen to or respect a word
she said, that they were secretly laughing at her authority
and conspiring to make her look foolish. Without realizing
it, she wound up antagonizing people who were basically
on her side and her fears became a self-fulfilling prophecy.

There are many reasons why an adolescent falls back
upon these early lessons. On the one hand an adolescent is
confronted with a variety of situations that he has to cope
with and that he has never experienced before. He has
never, for example, made love before. He has not evolved
any sexual techniques. He does not even know if a woman
will go to bed with him. He has no personal reassuring
evidence that he is an attractive, sexually competent male.
The first time he does so, however, the issue has gone a
long way toward being resolved. It is also a totally new
experience, which explains why so many people will always
remember the person with whom they lost their virginity.

The same holds true for many other areas, such as an adolescent's values. The quest for an identity never ceases. It continues throughout one's adult life. The older we become the more, it is hoped, we grow and consolidate our sense of who and what we are. As can be imagined, the first time one faces all these issues, when one is starting virtually from the ground up, the impact of the events and the decisions an adolescent confronts is especially profound and long lasting.

On the other hand, we neither enter the world at birth, or confront it during adolescence, as a blank slate. In the above example, a variety of unconscious impulses could well have impelled our young sexual initiate to have failed to "perform." Or even more seriously he could be at the mercy of impulses that somehow make him fend off women, perhaps inviting rejection in advance.

If we had to summarize an adolescent's "agenda" down to its essentials it would include:

- establishment of an individual separate identity
- the capacity to become involved in healthy intimate love relationships
- the capacity to function independently
- the ability to trust and to think well of oneself
- an appetite for growth and new experiences and to perform work that is both gratifying and meaningful.

The conflicts around and abilities to cope with those challenges as an adolescent were first formed many years before. This does not mean that the outcome must necessarily result in suicide. Still, when one mixes two highly volatile substances, which one's early childhood and one's adolescence often are, the results can be explosive.

The problem of how an adolescent experiences the pressure to be independent is a good example. One analyst, Peter Blos, has characterized this stage as parallel to the early stage when the child was two years old. Up until then the infant primarily thinks of himself and the world as one.

He feels that he is a part of everything and everything is a part of him. After the age of two, the child begins to recognize that there is an outside world apart from himself.

Burt had something very close to an ideal childhood environment. Around the age of two he had a good recognition of his boundaries, of where he left off and the rest of the world began. He was able to be aware of his sense of separateness, feeling emotionally secure and ready to accept it. He was his own little man; he constituted his own fascinating and unique world. It was a nice feeling.

Therefore, and this is oversimplifying things a bit to illustrate my point, when he next met up with the issue of being on his own he looked forward to it. He had a feeling that the adult world spread out before him like a vast, stupendous dream. There were new worlds to conquer. It was an opportunity for adventures.

By contrast there was Diane. At roughly the same age she survived a car crash that killed both her parents. The tragedy summarily separated her from her parents before she was emotionally prepared for separation. Her first experience with separation was extraordinarily traumatic and left her with an overwhelming feeling of being abruptly abandoned and left for dead. Although she was close enough to the grandparents who raised her, she was secretly petrified at the prospect of going away to college. Her relationships with boys were no less problematic.

She clung to them to the point that they rejected her in order to be able to breathe. These abandonments, on an unconscious level, reactivated her early and first abandonment. Each one became more shattering because it reconfirmed her belief that she would be deserted and left for dead precisely by those people she loved and depended upon most. She did finally go away to school at her grandparents' insistence. They felt that was the best way for her to ease into an independent existence.

Diane experienced going away to school as she had

learned to interpret related events in her life—as if she were unwanted. After one or two shaky, unsuccessful liaisons with freshman boys she took an overdose of barbiturates.

Burt and Diane are extreme examples. Most childhood and later adolescent experiences fall somewhere in between.

What is crucial here is that an adolescent is confronted with adult and quasi-adult situations that he must cope with. Often he does not have the mature and seasoned responses in his emotional repertoire because he has not had the exposure and the experience that adulthood brings. Instead he often tries to cope by falling back upon experiences from his distant past.

When a child learns to walk, for example, he begins to form possessive feelings toward one parent and feelings of jealousy and rage toward the other. Early and powerful feelings of initiative or guilt are forged. Much later, when a child first enters school, he develops a basic sense of industriousness and inferiority.

These stages, as laid out by author and psychoanalyst Erik Erikson, are some of the foundations an adolescent "instinctively" calls upon to orient himself or herself in the world. A child who learned to mistrust her father is likely to depend upon that lesson when facing boys for the first time. A boy who feels he failed to have his mother all to himself as a child because, irrationally, he believes he was not "good enough" will in many instances anticipate girls finding him a disappointment.

The more troubled an adolescent is the greater the probability these early stages are likely to erupt. Erikson points out that when one stage, for example that of industry and inferiority, is not fruitfully resolved, a person "gets stuck" in that stage. He or she carries that conflict up through the years like a millstone.

Freud provided an excellent analogy to understand this. He postulated that the development of the mind is comparable to an advancing army. As it moves forward it invariably meets with opposition. The advancing army meets the enemy and does battle in an effort to capture fresh territory. The more ferocious the battle, the more depleted the advancing forces become.

After securing the territory, the army's battle strength is further depleted by the troops it must leave behind at the recently captured garrison, which we may think of as a stage of emotional development.

It is the nature of armies to move forward, and as this one does, further and further drained by every full-pitch encounter, it may eventually meet with total defeat. When that happens the army retreats to that garrison, that stage of emotional development in which it is the most secure and strong. Freud's analogy, of course, like all analogies, is inexact. In this one each "enemy" or source of resistance is a new and more complex problem of coping. In day-to-day existence no clear-cut boundaries between garrisons exist. One phase of growth and resolution or irresolution blends into another.

With this theoretical background, we are now in a position to examine in detail the roots of the emotional difficulties of adolescents most susceptible to suicide. The seeds of an adolescent's sense of competence and self-confidence are planted, if they are planted, virtually from the moment of birth. The children of mothers who do not know how to nurture, soothe, and "merge" with them miss fundamental, indispensable experiences essential for the formation of a sturdy emotional foundation. Later on, as adolescents, they too often do not have the emotional capacity or skills, for example, to learn constructive lessons from life's stresses. Nor are they able to adapt to their environment or to other people in a way that will lead to healthy, satisfactory relationships.

When we use the term "inadequate mothering" we do not mean that these parents do not care for their children. In one sense mothering is a skill. Some mothers simply do not have that skill, often because they were never taught it by the example of their own mothering experiences. Nevertheless, when their offspring reach adolescence they often have special problems in making up for emotional voids. Their problems are equivalent to physical handicaps.

Why, for example, are some adolescents destined to plod through their lives, always trying to accomplish and succeed but never quite making it? What is the cause-and-effect scenario in their formative years that somehow is reinforced or reenacted in their social environment and by society itself much later? These are not children who are overwhelmed with feelings of intense misery and self-hatred. Yet they often decide to stop trying and end their lives.

A mother's ability to provide a healthy foundation is based upon an exquisite combination of how her body and her heart instinctively mesh with her child's needs. Human relationships, the relationship one forms to oneself, are systems just as the body itself is a system. How the system works, or breaks down, can best be brought to life by examining what the late eminent pediatrician, analyst, and author Donald Winnicott called "primary maternal preoccupation."

Normally it begins before the baby is born. Scientific evidence suggests that women who conceive possess levels of hormones that make them emotionally receptive and eager to care for children. Since a child's survival is directly dependent upon a mother's care, that obviously has crucial practical value. Anyone who has seen a mother with a newborn cannot help but be struck, during the first few days and weeks of its life, how absolutely and exclusively her attention is focused on her child.

In fact, the mother usually withdraws from the rest of the world, from her family and friends, to devote herself exclusively to the infant's needs, in effect to create an environment in which the child is the sun, the moon, and the stars. She "leaves reality" for a world in which only she and her child exist. Everyone else is excluded. Outsiders usually cannot help but be struck by the intense twenty-four-hour-a-day scope of her involvement. She seems to treat the child as though she were still carrying him, as if he were still a part of her body.

She eventually returns, of course, but during her withdrawal she is, practically speaking, in tune with her child's needs, instantly, absolutely, intuitively. She is, ideally, in a position to sense the baby's needs even before the baby is aware of them, before the child experiences the agitation and pain of hunger, soiled clothing, and so on.

What about mothers and infants in which this closeness does not exist? Why cannot some women nurture their infants in this fashion, and how does this lack lead to the plodding, ineffectual youngster who enters adolescence with great clumsiness, such as those we referred to earlier?

A patient of mine, a thirty-year-old woman, gave birth to a boy named Billy. Her own mother was a dynamic, powerful woman who ruled an industrial empire. She had virtually no time for her daughter, who was given over to a series of indifferent maids. Owing to her mother's tyrannical and demanding style, there was a continuous turnover of servants, and as a result the daughter never knew the experience of being nurtured and cared for by her own mother, or even by a true surrogate mother.

This amounted to a large emotional void, what professionals call a "trauma of omission," in her personality. As a result my patient approached motherhood with a very low opinion of its intrinsic value or its complexities. The way she saw it, one might say the way she had been raised to see it, was that "any animal can reproduce." Its sole function, therefore, was to continue the family line. Throughout her pregnancy she insisted that motherhood itself was a simple, straightforward procedure that would present positively no problems. She was rapidly reading through a number of child-raising manuals. She would raise her child "according to the books" and all would go well.

Already we can see that the emotional void in her own upbringing was so complete that her basic viewpoint was that child care was an unemotional, dry procedure to be done by the book. Shortly after she delivered Billy, she learned that her reading alone was inadequate. She coped with some situations, those the books covered, awkwardly and laboriously. Inevitably she was confronted with a host of problems that did not represent themselves chapter by chapter but simultaneously; she could neither anticipate nor find them in the index. Where intuition and ingenuity were needed, she was at a complete loss. It simply was never conveyed to her and it was not a part of her natural makeup.

For all her good intentions she could not help but communicate her plodding, clumsy, ineffectual ministrations to her child. Regular, continual, smooth feedings proved impossible for her. Not because she was negligent; rather, she did not have a "feel" for when Billy ought to be fed. The unnatural difficulties she encountered in such routine chores as bottle washing, diaper changing, and bathing forced her to postpone the main task of feeding the baby. The regular cycle of nurturing that an infant needs to feel at home in the world was never established. As can be imagined, my patient had so many problems meeting Billy's relatively straightforward basic physical needs that when it came to the vital nuances of emotional care, Billy always suffered. She was astonished, for example, when she saw how delighted her friend's infant was over playing a game of peek-a-boo with her mother. No one had ever played this game with her when she was a child and she had literally never seen it before. Obviously Billy was deprived of that sort of care and play, which serves a very important purpose.

As it happened, Billy grew up feeling that somehow nothing came easily, neither putting himself together properly when he got dressed nor playing in a comfortable give-and-take with his school chums, nor catching on in school and learning how to do his homework properly. He managed to get by, but doing so always required a laborious, draining, inefficient effort, which he executed in a clumsy, awkward, unsatisfying way.

The sense of ineffectuality, of never being quite with it, slowly became unbearable when he had to face the imponderables of who he was and how he was going to get on in the world. Without knowing quite why, he came home from a mixer one evening in early fall and leapt out his second-floor bedroom window. Fortunately, he survived and was subsequently able to resolve some of the inbred feelings of ineffectuality with professional help.

Another group of adolescents particularly susceptible to suicide are those who feel profoundly alienated, from both themselves and the world around them. Everyone is alienated from the world to some degree. As with all broad, generalized groupings we draw, we use the term "susceptible" to suicide quite intentionally. Adolescents routinely feel clumsy and awkward in some circumstances, just as they often feel profoundly alienated in others. Having such feelings does not make someone automatically suicidal.

Children who have incorporated little of an inner sense of security during childhood find they feel wholly and intensely unable to fit in anywhere in the adult world during adolescence. This, for all the built-in societal pressures that alienate people, is a condition that does not arise intellectually. It is an intense, vaguely articulated kind of pain that a child brings to the difficulties of adolescence.

But why? How does a child learn, or not learn, ways of adapting to life that will make life relatively comfortable?

Again, we find the answers in one's earliest childhood. The problems that begin in what is known as the "symbiotic" phase of infancy often amount to the first seeds of what later results in a suicide attempt.

The term "symbiotic phase" means nothing more than the period in which a child and his mother are so wholly involved with each other that they seem to have a mutual dependence. They are dependent upon each other for survival and meet each other's needs in a complementary way. The phrase is somewhat inexact, since an infant is far more helpless than a mother. Still, it does convey the intensity of the attachment.

Up until two months of age an infant experiences other people as nothing more than functions that gratify needs and bring about relief from inner tension. After that the child begins to have a dim perception of his mother as both a part of him, an extension of himself, as well as another human being.

If this sounds unusual or difficult to accept, one need only recall the feelings of idyllic love and union, common during adolescence, in which we experience contented bliss. Remnants of these feelings linger on in the fantasies we all have about the raptures of love we would enjoy with "the perfect mate."

Novelist Tom Berger described the essence of what we are focusing on in a scene from his novel *Little Big Man*. In it the protagonist, after a period of lovemaking in the open air, expresses his feeling of being in total harmony with himself and the universe thusly:

> All seemed right to me at that moment. It was one of the few times I felt: this is the way things are and should be. . . . *I knew where the center of the world was.* A remarkable feeling, in which time turns in a circle and he who stands at the core has power over everything that takes the form of line and square and angle. [Italics added.]

For an infant at this stage the sense of what comes from inside and what comes from outside is blurred. The baby believes that everything that happens to him, for better or for worse, could just as well come from within as from without. The boundaries themselves are only dimly apprehended, if apprehended at all.

Ideally a mother at this time is so in tune with her in-

fant's needs that she anticipates and responds before the
child senses or anticipates his own needs. In other words,
the cycle of waking and sleep, hunger and satiety, which at
this point encompasses virtually the whole range of an infant's experiences of the world, is satisfied in such a profound, consistent, and regular fashion that the infant believes his sense of harmony and well-being is coming from
within himself.

As far as the infant experiences his world, he is not terribly aware that he is dependent upon anyone. Without
moving a muscle, so to speak, he is continually gratified and
at peace.

A mother—especially at this point—is a person's first and
most important teacher. She embodies the nature of the
world. It is from her that an infant learns whether the world
is a soothing or a hostile place, whether the infant fits comfortably within it, is in harmony with it or not.

If all goes well in these first days in which he begins to
form a sense of identity, an infant knows—at a visceral level
—that he is secure in a world in which he will be taken
care of. On the one hand infants feel that they are nurturing
themselves, which translates later into feelings of self-confidence and self-esteem. They just know they are good, competent, likable people who enjoy who they are. They know
they are able to take care of themselves and do not need
others to compensate for their emotional gaps.

They experience the needs they have without great anxiety. Their needs reawaken memories of past situations when
those needs were satisfactorily met. *Since they have known
gratification in the past, they can anticipate it in the future.*

Hunger, for example, leaves them feeling eager for a good
hearty meal rather than agitated. Separation from a parent
does not overwhelm them with feelings of loneliness, anxiety, and desertion. Inside, somehow, the caring parent is
always "with them." They can feel comfortable when alone
and eagerly anticipate a happy reunion.

As children grow up they begin to expand and explore the world around them. They have new experiences and relationships other than those with their mother. The children raised in the ideal fashion we have described generally tend to be open, self-confident, and warm. For them the world is an unthreatening, supportive place in which to indulge their curiosity and give it free play. When they meet with hostility or rejection it does not match their own feelings about themselves and so they can more easily shrug it off. In the core of their being they feel in harmony with themselves and, generally speaking, with the world around them. In the beginning the world adapted to them and later on they were able to learn to adapt comfortably to the world.

Others are not so fortunate. For them life is inordinately difficult. These are the adolescents who simply cannot tolerate the excruciating pain of being alone. Nor does human contact soothe them. They feel tremendously uneasy, alienated in the company of others. They cannot be alone and they cannot be secure and intimately trustful.

For them the world is a threatening, overbearing, malevolent place. They may get along well in school, but new situations leave them terrified and they shrink from even the prospect of placing themselves in a fresh atmosphere, such as a ski trip organized by their high school. Without realizing it they deny themselves important experiences and relationships in order to preserve the comfortable and the familiar and fend off anticipated pain and threats, and in the long run they box themselves into positions of helplessness and vulnerability.

Such was the case with Alex, who, though raised in a generally caring and well-intentioned household, endured a terribly frustrating and difficult early childhood. He was a firstborn, and as is often the case, his mother let her lack of experience and self-confidence get the upper hand.

Believing the experts knew best, she fed him according

to a preplanned schedule. When she did feed him, it was done in a tense and anxious spirit.

Alex's father did not hide the resentment he felt over the drastic drop in attention he received from his wife during Alex's early infancy. He was the provider, and her job as wife included, in his mind, striking a more "evenhanded balance" between his demands on her attention and her son's. Alex's mother, a good-natured and compliant sort, devoted superhuman energies trying to keep everyone happy.

Somehow Alex learned to experience his first needs, his hunger and other needs, as painful sources of anxiety that the world was in no great rush to respond to. The needs themselves became threatening and the frustrations and difficulties he associated with getting them met left him feeling that dependency was something to be feared, that independence meant isolation, and that the persons he cared about most were the very ones least likely to understand and appreciate him.

As might be expected, one could hardly have met a more timid and insecure fifteen-year-old than Alex. He was no gawkier than his schoolmates but was convinced that only he felt that way. The usual rough teasing that children inflict on one another at that age had a devastating effect upon him. It matched his own negative feelings about himself and it made human contact a source of torture.

Having no confidence that his parents would have any empathy or understanding for how he felt, he did not consider sharing his anguish with them. Indeed they saw him as the apple of their eye, an adolescent who was undergoing the normal growing pains, and with their rose-colored glasses firmly in place, they failed to recognize his serious distress.

Alex was a good student but had it in his head that the regular nine-to-five adult working world was one enormous dungeon in which none of his needs for independence and making a meaningful contribution would be allowed. He normally came home directly after school, shunning all ex-

tracurricular activities. While his parents thought him simply a "late bloomer," Alex found social life only height-
ened his sense of not belonging.

So, acting in what they thought were his best interests,
his parents insisted Alex attend an after-school vocational
seminar. At one point a counselor asked Alex to tell the
group what his interests were. Alex, put on the spot, stam-
mered in embarrassment and confusion. Without thinking,
he blurted out, "I don't have any."

Thinking to ease Alex's discomfort and establish a rap-
port with him, the counselor stared theatrically at the girls
around the room and said, "Not even one?"

The group broke out in laughter. Alex felt deeply humiliated. Instead of making him feel at ease, the counselor, in
Alex's mind, was ridiculing him. He was publicly deriding
him for his timidity and lack of success with girls, something
he assumed everyone else in the room, based on their laughter, also must have felt about him.

Although the remark was soon forgotten, Alex sat down
almost in tears. He endured his agitation as long as he could
and then unobtrusively got up and left. At the corner drugstore he bought a packet of razor blades and returned home.
There, while his father was working late at the office and
his mother was attending a teacher's meeting, Alex found
the only relief from his torment he could conceive of, in
death.

Having discussed the self-destructive urges that afflict two
of the largest and most typical suicidal groups, whom we
may broadly label the ineffectual and the alienated, we shall
focus on a third group before moving on to the current
problems presented by our society.

This group we can call the agitated. Those are the youngsters who appear volatile, frenzied, and gripped by uncontrollable nervous energy. Everyone is caught up in those
emotional states at various points in his life. Normally they
are related to or evoked by some immediate and passing

difficulty. If, for example, an adolescent had set her heart on making the cheerleading squad, achieving an A in her history class, and waiting for a call from the most popular boy in her class, she would be less than human if she were not on pins and needles.

In this case her nervous energy has a specific, and one might even say a constructive, focus. The group I shall discuss are just "naturally" agitated. Their nervous energy takes on either destructive or seemingly meaningless forms. They are, in a sense, possessed by agitation.

The causes for this underscore a crucial insight into adolescent behavior, one I shall be returning to again and again. That is, that the way someone sees himself and experiences the world is based upon the original atmosphere he knew. That original atmosphere, no matter what it is, represents security and familiarity. The fear of the unknown is usually one of the greatest sources of anxiety mankind has. People learn to adapt to the world, to defend themselves against it based upon the frame of mind (in the widest sense) they instinctively associate with the kind of person they are. Adolescents have an enormous need for security and familiarity because they are faced with so much uncertainty. What agitated teenagers teach us—though they are certainly not the only ones who do this—is that *no matter how painfully unhappy they feel, if it corresponds to their state of mind in "the infantile atmosphere" it provides a sense of security and familiarity they cannot live without and which they cannot enjoy under any other condition.*

A case in point would be of a mother and her daughter Felicia. The mother had married into a well-to-do family on Chicago's suburban North Shore. She entered psychiatric treatment at her family's insistence when her daughter was about twelve.

She was a restless, tense woman who, among other emotional difficulties, was concerned about her daughter. At one point in her treatment her therapist expressed his curiosity as to how she fed and soothed her daughter as an infant.

She began tentatively but soon grew comfortable enough in the therapeutic setting to become totally immersed in her style of mothering, the only one she knew.

Even for a therapist it was a painful thing to witness. For the woman simply had no idea what a cruel parody of nurturing she had made her own. She went through the motions of roughly grasping her daughter. Whereas most mothers would make warm, playful, cooing expressions dance across their faces, she made elaborate and rather frightening grimaces. Her cooing itself sounded like a painful, dissonant wail.

When most mothers are about to feed their children they gently lift them up, tenderly arrange them in their arms so that the child's head receives the requisite support, and surround the breast-feeding ritual with soft, soothing murmurs. Their natural instinct, in short, provides an all-enveloping warm environment.

This mother, though attempting to provide that for her child, produced quite opposite results. In the office she went through the motions of picking up her daughter by abruptly seizing her by the waist. While talking in a staccato fashion to the therapist she swung the symbolic infant in a wide arc and then laid her very heavily against the arm normally used to hold the bottle. She forced the bottle into the infant's mouth and jiggled it up and down in a clumsy, jarring fashion.

She began to hum, but it was a piercing, unpleasant noise. In what she apparently thought to be soothing and relaxing gestures she began rapidly to poke her imaginary child with her index finger all over her body.

Obviously Felicia's mother had no idea of what she was really doing to her child. The emotional mood she inspired in her, which is just as important as physical nutrition, was

painful, disruptive, and agitating. Instead of being a soothing, calming experience, the security of feeding became associated with something chaotic and upsetting. The long-
range consequence of that, though again I am simplifying
the complex process of human development to stress a point,
was that Felicia came to feel most comfortable when she
was agitated.

The first experience of "calming" became the model for
all later ones. Felicia grew up to be what we would now
call "hyper." At the age of sixteen she was known among
her friends as someone in constant, frantic activity that had
no constructive purpose. Nothing seemed able to bring her
to anything approaching a serene state.

Her daily routine would begin around 5:00 A.M. since she
was so anxious to get a head start on the day, or rather to
keep from falling behind. It would take her forty-five minutes to choose her day's outfit, going nervously and chaot-
ically from drawer to drawer, opening and shutting them
without being able to come to any final decision, her mind
racing a mile an agitated minute.

She would remove a pair of socks and then put them
back. Walking quickly to her closet she would choose a
blouse, run her fingers along the creases, than hang it back
up, flicking off invisible specks of lint in the process. Next,
she would change her mind and remove the blouse again,
get one arm inside a sleeve and then remove it and return
it to the closet for fear it would not go with the skirt she
had in mind. All of this was done, of course, at an intense
pace that would have exhausted anyone.

The ensuing day in school was nothing more than a vari-
ation on this theme. Despite having awakened so early, she
somehow managed to leave the house late. The walk to the
school building then also fit in with her early picture of
security, that is, it was an anxiety-riddled ordeal. Once there,
her learning experience was a series of frantic searches for

misplaced assignments and frenetic attempts to find the appropriate passages in the assigned texts.

Whenever she was called upon in class she answered in a scattered, nervous, nearly incoherent way. A conversation with a boy during lunch period was enough to send her into a chattering frenzy, correcting and contradicting almost any opinion she expressed and totally reversing field and reexplaining what she really meant if the young fellow happened to express a somewhat different point of view.

To outsiders, it might have seemed that Felicia was a somewhat scatterbrained girl, a vulnerable, frantic adolescent vaguely reminiscent of the "screwball comediennes" of the thirties movie era.

The truth was that Felicia suffered enormously from her agitation. Never to know a moment's peace, or rather, to have the only peace you know bring with it a constant driving agitation, would be enough to drive some people to the breaking point. In this case, unfortunately, it did. By the time she was seventeen, Felicia was dead from an overdose of sleeping pills.

It would be wrong to blame Felicia's mother for her daughter's death. Many factors were involved and the early environment is important. It is true that there are parents who contribute, although unconsciously, to their children's suicide. It is a tragic problem, an ever recurring one that I will be discussing in chapter 7.

It is very important to keep in mind that suicide is the end product of a variety of forces. It is possible that Felicia was so scarred by her early experience that nothing could have saved her. It is far more likely that if a friend, a relative, a teacher, or a therapist had been able to intervene, the tragedy could have been averted.

The important lesson for us here is that early on adolescents learn ways in which they are able to soothe themselves. If their first soothing experiences were inadequate, they often cannot enjoy and appreciate truly soothing experiences later in life. In Felicia's case a quiet room, soothing music, or even the rhythmic pounding of the seaside made her feel as though she were dead inside. The quiet was intolerable.

Let us conclude with a disturbing, though far less apocalyptic anecdote.

In this instance we are dealing with alcoholism. This mother came from a family of alcoholics. By the time her son Frank was an adolescent she too suffered from this disturbance. She awoke around noon, hung over, and met with her friends at a local restaurant, where she would drink until four. She would return home and continue drinking. When her family came home in the evening she was invariably dead drunk.

Like many alcoholics, she denied her addiction. In fact, she had quite strong—and positive—feelings about temperance. She was quite adamant that there was nothing more revolting, undignified, and unladylike than an alcoholic housewife, which she made it a point never to become.

When she entered treatment, at her family's insistence, it became clear to me that alcohol was as indispensable to her as oxygen. She needed it to calm her inner agitation.

Her son Frank, at the age of thirteen, was already emotionally mired in the psychic (as opposed to the biological) inheritance he had received. He was a constantly anxious young boy, so restless he literally could not sit still. He was almost expelled from junior high school for his disruptive behavior. By the time he reached high school, he was showing up drunk or bleary-eyed from liquor and barbiturates.

While drunk Frank was loud, vociferous, obscene, and destructive. He went through a variety of boarding schools, where he was expelled over and over for his drinking problem, and where he invariably got into one kind of self-destructive accident or another. Usually these involved traffic mishaps.

Fortunately Frank received treatment, and the pattern of his behavior, its sources and its strategy soon became clear. Without realizing it, he had emulated and adopted his mother's means of coping.

Frank drank to calm himself. Without drinking, he suffered from tension that mounted to an unbearable intensity. The only way he could protect himself from it was to anesthetize himself with alcohol.

As for antisocial behavior, that too had a positive meaning for him. Like his mother, Frank adopted this way of emotionally insulating himself from an alien world. He would, typically, relax in a chair, stare out the window, and leisurely blow smoke rings in the therapist's general direction in order to display his contempt and indifference.

Just in case the doctor failed to get the message, Frank ignored all but a few of the therapist's questions and observations. When he did respond, he was condescending. In this he was very much like his alcoholic mother. Like her, he too acted oblivious to the people around him. The contemptuousness and the obliviousness both had the same purpose, to insulate himself from a threatening world.

On one occasion, however, Frank revealed a recurring and very revealing fantasy. He envisioned himself sitting in a war tank parked on a beach during the winter. The ocean was partially frozen. He sat there contemptuously smoking as two enemy soldiers vainly tried to break in. What delighted him most was how infuriated they were because they were not able to enter the tank and take him prisoner. He was, in his eyes, insulated and invulnerable.

Without realizing it consciously, Frank was expressing the essence of his emotional cage. Most people naturally want to communicate and share their moments of great happiness or pain (is that not what an infant first learns to do when gaining physical and emotional sustenance from a mother?).

Who among us yearns, as author Harry Mark Petrakis put

it, "to exist like barricaded islands in the midst of multi-tudes, fearful or unwilling to reveal ourselves or to dis-cover the meaning of others"?

Yet for Frank, people evoked in him the gnawing agi-tation he could only escape while "on a sheet of ice." Hav-ing never known true peace, the closest he could come to it was freezing everyone out, including himself.

In many ways, unfortunately, that is what our society is also doing to our adolescents, driving them in some cases to a very different kind of oblivion.

CHAPTER 3

Who Are We?

> The world has prepared no place for you and if the
> world had its way no place would ever exist. Now this is
> true for everyone but . . . this is not the way this truth
> presents itself to [those] who believe the world is theirs
> and who, albeit unconsciously, expect the world to help
> them in the achievement of their identity. But the world
> does not do this—for anyone; the world is not interested
> in anyone's identity.
>
> JAMES BALDWIN

MONTEFEGATESI IS A REMOTE RURAL VILLAGE in the Italian
province of Tuscany. The village has been in existence for
centuries and its roughly one thousand residents, up until
recently, had remained essentially untouched by modern
technology and the social revolution it normally involves.

The community was a series of large extended families
with traditional values and roles. Concepts of commercial,
sexual, social, and religious duties were what we would call
"old world." It was a patriarchal society in which the man
was the undisputed head of the household. Women were
housewives and mothers. Montefegatesi was, as it always had
been, an agricultural community in which a man had, for
all practical purposes, the choice of being either a farmer
or a tradesman.

About ten years ago, I visited Montefegatesi. I was curious
about the way the young men of the village saw themselves
and the world around them and what sorts of ambitions

they had. They were, of course, aware of the different kinds
of lives being led in the major cities of Italy and therefore
the different sorts of opportunities potentially open to them.

Why, I asked one adolescent shepherd, with the whole
world open to you, do you choose simply to raise sheep?

Why? he replied. Because that is what I am, a shepherd.
My father was a shepherd and his father before him. It is
what I was born to do.

In the winter of 1979 I was invited to deliver an address
at a psychiatric conference in Guatemala City. While by no
means as static a society as that of the above village, Guatemala City retains many social features all but unknown in
the largest American metropolises.

I knew very little about how closely urban Central American society resembled our own, and it was something I
was naturally curious about. Even so, my instincts told me
that urban life is fundamentally the same everywhere.

One Guatemalan colleague soon brought me up short. I
had asked him where he had received his training, and when
he told me, I asked him what it was like being young, foot-
loose, and totally on your own at the time.

"But in our country one never severs one's ties with one's
family," he replied.

"But what about when you go away to school?"

"You attend a college within easy distance to your home,
which is where you normally live while pursuing your
studies."

"But what about when you get married?"

"Your family may build an extension onto their own
house so that you may move in with them. Otherwise you
live very nearby."

"But what about your job? Doesn't that ever take you
far away?"

"In most every case no. You are a close part of your family from the day you're born to the day you die. That is

how it is, that is what most people anticipate, and for the most part the feeling is that that is how it should be."

The director of a large mental hospital in Moscow came to this country not long ago to attend an international conference. After delivering her paper she took questions from the floor, and one analyst asked her if they had a high proportion of suicides and drug addiction among their adolescent population.

"No," she answered calmly. "Alcoholism is our main problem. Drugs and suicide, no, not yet. I expect these to become problems when Russia becomes more materialistic in the sense that America is. When Coca-Cola, the Hilton hotels, and all the other forms of Western mass life-style take firm and pervasive root in our country, then I believe the incidence of drug problems and adolescent suicide will begin to become a major, major problem."

Most of us, to say the least, would have a great deal of difficulty fitting comfortably into any of these cultures. Or, to put it another way, most of us would violently dismiss anyone mad enough to suggest seriously that we as a society come to a complete and sudden stop in order to reorganize our culture to make it a duplicate of those we have just described. To us it would mean an intolerable impingement on our personal freedom. Besides, these other cultures, from our point of view, are "obsolete," "anachronisms."

In Montefegatesi, for example, the whole way in which young people defined their lives, the way in which they framed and executed their goals, would be irrelevant. There are no institutions and mechanisms by which they can be trained for, and then pursue, professional careers.

The lack of opportunity for improving one's social and economic status would be suffocating to us.

As with this little Italian village, Guatemala City would also impose unbearable restrictions from our point of view.

What is the use of living in America if we cannot escape the confines of our family? Most of us would be outraged if we were expected to submit absolutely to the will of a patriarch, a father, a grandfather, a priest, or a minister.

The time is over, we hope, never to return, when it would call a woman's sexual identity into question if she decided to forego housework for a commercial career. ERA opponents aside, who would voluntarily welcome a society in which women were acknowledged as subordinate, less capable beings?

Most Americans have struggled very hard to release themselves from the old-world moralities. Whether or not professional successes, wealth, prestige, and material comforts can, or were intended to, replace those strictures as the center of our lives, hardly anyone today would want to turn back the clock. The prospect of being answerable to someone else for the way in which we decide to conduct our private life is not a treasured one among us.

On the other hand, whatever else one can say about those societies, they are not plagued by crime, slums, drugs, pollution, and adolescent suicide. Perhaps as adults we would not be comfortable in those societies, but the adolescents who belong to them are moderately comfortable. Our adolescents are by and large painfully uncomfortable.

It sounds odd at first, but one of the very first lessons we can extract from the juxtaposition of our culture with others is that the increased incidence of adolescent suicide in America is a recent development that paradoxically implies some very positive things.

It serves to isolate the problems involved and steers us away from misconceptions we—and that includes professionals in the psychiatric field—evolve from lack of perspective.

Of course no sensitive and thoughtful adult can fail to be alarmed by the tragic waste of human life and human potential that the rising incidence represents. Nothing could be more counterproductive than taking a rose-colored view of this urgent matter.

Human beings all over the globe have been able to help adolescents make the transition to adulthood in very large numbers for hundreds, if not thousands, of years. There is no basis, therefore, for believing our current problem of adolescent suicide is immutable, something beyond our abilities to remedy.

The fact that this is one of the first books to address this problem indicates that adults have not wanted to face it because it is so very painful and disturbing. Our guilt must be related to specific, identifiable reasons that in some ways are peculiar to our society and that are responsible for the epidemic of youthful self-destruction.

The low or nonexistent incidence in other cultures should, first of all, reassure us that the self-destructive urge is not biologically predetermined. That is, a person inherits a gene for brown eyes or baldness or flat feet, but as far as we know no one is born with a gene that condemns him to suicide.

Some clinicians in this country define adolescence itself as a species of psychopathology and therefore a stage of human development that, by its very nature, is especially susceptible to suicide. Other cultures and other eras did not generally have this problem. That is a very useful piece of information. It tells us that, in fact, our society, at the present time, is failing to supply adolescents with a number of crucial supports other societies routinely delivered.

Why, for example, do our adolescents seem so obsessed by the question, Who am I? A parent may well find this dilemma difficult to appreciate. A parent sees his child acquire a personality and certain aptitudes. He knows who his child is and perhaps it is natural to assume his offspring should be able to perceive himself with similar clarity.

Why are not some adolescents in other cultures plagued by that same existential question? How can adults appreciate the force behind an adolescent's most common crisis? How does our society reinforce the earlier emotional instabilities suicidal adolescents bring to these years? What exactly are the missing pieces in their environment?

In earlier eras people did not spend the first twenty years of their lives as dependents. This is one peculiarity of adolescence in the United States. Here, a child is expected to turn himself into an adult while, in the meantime, he is totally dependent upon his elders, who may or may not be able to provide the kinds of vocational role models an adolescent seeks for adulthood.

In what we would call primitive cultures, such as the American Cheyenne Indians, people did of course live through and beyond what we consider the adolescent years, but the narrowness, or what we could consider constriction, of their roles, hunter and warrior, was in one respect an advantage.

For, as with the Tuscan shepherds, the young children were never basically overwhelmed with confusion over who they were or what kind of person they ought to strive to be.

From virtually the time a Cheyenne boy was capable of walking, for example, he was responsible for rising before the rest of his tribe and, with the other boys, tending to the ponies, a very precious resource of the Cheyenne adults. After a morning bath the young boys would often gather bows and tipless arrows and play war. This could be followed by some wrestling.

The next activity also mimicked and trained them for their coming adult responsibilities. Young girls would set up miniature tepees and boys, pretending to be husbands, would go on mock war parties and mock buffalo hunts in which they got in a little more target practice.

As they grew older they underwent initiation rights and were formally received as adults and as equals.

In earlier societies children were valued in different and very important ways. Their passage from childhood to adulthood was a continuous, unbroken progression. While in some sense they were dependent, they were not, practically speaking, irrelevant and valueless. Everyone had a job to perform that was an important contribution to the family's overall welfare. Their childhoods were designed to equip them for an honored role in society from the very beginning.

Rather than finding it confining, adolescents in these cultures, although this is not to say that they lived pleasure-filled, untraumatic existences, found the structure reassuring. They had a stable environment within which they could work out their uncertainties over whether they would eventually make successful warriors, mothers, shepherds, and other roles. They also had strong family units with strong authority figures to model themselves upon, fathers whose occupation was dignified and enhanced by the long tradition behind it, parents who could set clear-cut goals for their children to achieve and could take clear and unmistakable pride in their eventual successes.

Today, adolescents have the same human needs and longings, but it is obviously a very different world. Unlike their historical equivalents, they are occupants of a stage of life that amounts more or less to a limbo. They are not children and they are not adults.

When they attempt to act like adults, and this may range from anything from asking for the car keys to dropping out of school to be self-supporting, they are routinely reminded that they are children who cannot make those kinds of decisions on their own. When they act like moody, mercurial children, they are often upbraided by being told they ought to act like adults.

At this point some readers might interject, Yes, all that is very true. But, after all, isn't that what adolescence is for, a period stretching over several years in which an adolescent can occupy himself with these very questions, a rather lengthy period in which he is permitted to experiment with different activities until he strikes upon the right one for him? If that is so, should not today's adolescents have an advantage over previous generations, who did not have what we might consider to be a respite from adult responsibility?

It would be ideal, of course, if that is how most adolescents viewed, or more importantly how they experienced, this stage in their lives.

It is true that adolescents are supposed to be occupied with these questions. They need, above all, to build a world around them in which they feel comfortable and valued and useful. In reality, groping through a limitless thicket of possible career choices and possible ethics and life-styles leaves many adolescents feeling lost at sea.

The problem is compounded, according to the eminent psychoanalyst and author Bruno Bettelheim, because in our society youth is obsolete. That might sound confusing at first. All the evidence of advertising and newspaper features pages points to our being a youth-oriented society. Adults, in theory anyway, are supposed to envy and long for youth above all things.

The people who actually constitute our country's youth do not see themselves as the centerpiece of their culture. It is no coincidence that it is adults who are overheard wishing that they were back in college again, while adolescents are more likely to apologize for being there, claiming that it is not the real world.

Bettelheim makes a quite telling point: There is no place for adolescents, as adolescents, in our technologically advanced society. They do not have the skills to function within it. They are perfectly aware that the underside of the precept that adolescence is a time for finding yourself is that during this period of their lives they are in fact superfluous people.

The very fact that today's teenagers are consumed by the questions, Who am I? What is the purpose of my life? What is meaningful? underscores how overwhelming so-called freedom can be.

Adolescents, to be sure, need all the help they can get from their parents and teachers in assisting them in discovering who they are.

Yet, in some ways, adults are in a peculiarly difficult position to do so. Those who grew up during or around the Depression, for example, had a very different orientation toward life.

Many were the sons and daughters of immigrant families. These were usually closely knit, or at least closely bound, extended groups with a strong, cohesive cultural tradition behind them. In their own minds, each ethnic group had a very strong identity of their own and a system of values and prejudices that told them who they were and how the world is. Whether they had a monopoly on undiluted, absolute truth is beside the point.

The imported immigrant culture was preserved for at least one generation in physically and psychologically self-contained neighborhoods. It provided self-definition and a system of values upon which American-born children could anchor their own sense of who they were as well as their need to form a separate, independent identity, in this case as assimilated Americans. Even if it were nothing more than something to belittle and reject at the time, it was there.

As best-selling author Mario Puzo lovingly wrote about his own transition:

I had every desire in the world to go wrong but I never had a chance. The Italian family structure was too formidable. I never came home to an empty house; there was always the smell of supper cooking. My mother was always there to greet me, sometimes with a policeman's club (nobody ever knew how she acquired it). But she was always there or her authorized deputy, my older sister. [Even so] it did seem then [as an adolescent] that the Italian immigrants, all the fathers and mothers I knew, were a grim lot, always shouting, always angry, quicker to quarrel than embrace. I did not understand that their lives were a long labor to earn their daily bread and that physical fatigue does not sweeten human natures.

Puzo underscores another important point: The struggle to make ends meet was paramount. Immigrant children were routinely expected to contribute to their family's survival with whatever odd or menial jobs they could find. As is so often the case, the deprivations of poverty, by present American living standards at least, inspired a determination to make money, "to make good." Poverty is frequently associated with serious emotional damage, but in many cases it stimulated these adolescents to pursue clear-cut, if not crude, goals.

Most of today's adolescents do not have these firmly rooted reference points. For many Americans the ethnic subworld is a thing of the past. With it died old-world moral imperatives. The structure of the family itself is changing. The single-parent household, a well near nonexistent phenomenon even fifteen years ago, is now common. As recent studies have shown, physical fights between parents, broken homes, exhibitionistic sexual activity witnessed by children, child abuse, and child neglect are not the sole province of the poor, as many have traditionally thought. They are pervasive today on all levels of our society, and that includes the so-called privileged.

Parents often forget that their own idealistic dreams had to be squelched during the Depression. They sublimated, or put aside, their own dreams to deal with the immediate material problems at hand—money, acceptance, and prestige.

Now, freed from those demands, their own children are thrust into a society that has fluid and poorly defined norms. The adolescent needs something to believe in, something with deep, enduring value. In our society he finds little to believe in.

There is an old proverb that says the spirit can roam only after the belly is full. Many adolescents are well fed physically. But where is their spirit? At a stage in their lives in which they are expected to evolve a system of values and ideals that is to last them the rest of their lives, they live in a society that is, for them, relatively valueless.

An adolescent is usually unable to perceive it, but most adults know that the idealistic jobs in America, the helping jobs (e.g., social work, community activism), pay next to nothing, and in this society money is a measure of importance. These idealistic jobs, as we shall see in the conclusion of the book, can be indispensable for an adolescent in crisis.

This society does not place tremendous emphasis on idealistic endeavor. What we emphasize is commerce. As R. J. Hollingdale observed in a brilliant essay on philosopher Arthur Schopenhauer, "the capitalistic world, and in particular the heart of it, the world of buying and selling, offers almost nothing a young man wants."

Schopenhauer himself lived during the Victorian era, a time in which we assume there were very few adolescents who committed suicide. Freud, who lived in mid-Victorian times, was confronted by adolescents with very different problems.

It was an age in which roles were largely predetermined and the social order—despite the inhuman restraints and repressions it imposed—was solid. By contrast, our society is so unstructured, so fluid as to be nearly the essence of instability. As a classic study by sociologist Emile Durkheim pointed out, the incidence of suicide in *any society rises with the degree of mounting instability*. By instability, Durkheim means change, not only from bad to good, but from good to bad as well.

Proof of just how unstable our society is, and in our case it has little to do with economic-social class uprisings, can be found in the ready acceptance author Alvin Toffler's *Future Shock* received. The book pointed out that the rate of technological change is so rapid that almost none of us is able to keep pace with it. This is one reason, incidentally, why our society also finds it difficult to cope with "useless"

retired elderly, as well as those middle-aged businessmen
who lose their jobs in the prime of life and are considered
by other industries "unemployable" because they cannot,
supposedly, retool themselves for jobs that did not even exist when they first entered the marketplace.

Schopenhauer, himself, though an exception to the rule
in his time, endured an adolescent identity crisis almost
any modern American adolescent can recognize. His case
underscores beautifully why today's youth find it so difficult,
and sometimes impossible, to find a meaningful place in
our society.

At the age of seventeen Schopenhauer's father died, while
his mother and sister moved to another city, leaving him to
a job as a clerk in a large mercantile concern.

As Hollingdale put it, in this "crucial epoch of his life
he begins to hate the mercantile world while his very modest
education has fitted him for little else. . . . and he is only
seventeen. . . . [By contrast] Dickens' experience [as a child
laborer] was that of a little boy unable to analyze his situation while Schopenhauer's is perhaps the common lot of
middle-class youth.

"The instincts of youth are at variance with the demands
of business," Hollingdale points out. "What young man is
by nature diligent, sober and regular in his habits? Respect-
ful to 'superiors' and humble before wealth? Sincerely able
to devote himself to what he finds boring? One in ten thousand perhaps . . . short of a total revolution in the conduct
of human affairs any conceivable social order will for the
great majority mean the boredom of routine, the damming
up of their natural energies and the frustration of their
natural desires. This familiar feeling was what now overcame
Schopenhauer: the feeling which appears when life hitherto
apparently capable of granting anything is suddenly revealed as a deception, when the colour is drained from it
and the whole future seems a single grey.

"The essence is in the question *Is this all? Is this* life?" [Italics added.]

By and large, then, our competitive and highly materialistic society is basically unequipped to accept, let alone channel constructively, the enormous fund of idealism and energy adolescents bring to society.

Most of us have resigned ourselves (some would say adjusted ourselves) more or less to a highly regulated existence designed to earn us a living, provide for others, and keep us alive. If we enjoy our work, all the better. If not, well, "it's a living." We have learned to define ourselves, to some degree, by our capacity for generosity, our hobbies, our family roles. That is, if we do not make our living according to our original dreams we learn to define and gratify ourselves outside our jobs. Our pride in material acquisitions is really, for many, a substitution for more grandiose accomplishments that life routinely denies us. Having met with our share of indifference and disappointment at the hands of the real world, having struggled to survive a world that is not concerned with our survival, the gratification of material well-being is derived from its symbolic significance. It is a symbol of the triumph over brutal struggle. It is a complex, difficult achievement. It does not take place overnight, or without, usually, a great deal of anguish.

A new car, an opulent house, extravagant jewelry we must remember have no intrinsic value. To one degree or another it is we who assign them their value.

Adolescents, on the other hand, are at a stage in their lives in which, as the clichés go, "Their whole lives are ahead of them." "They can be whatever they want to be."

Would most of us, if we had to plot out the rest of our lives from the beginning, choose to be, in essence, consumers of material indulgences? To feel worthwhile, important, someone who has made an impact on the world, someone who has a life to look forward to, adolescents generally need to occupy a position that provides them with intrinsically meaningful work.

Poet T. S. Eliot was not an adolescent when he wrote, "We are the hollow men / We are the stuffed men." He was speaking about the meaninglessness of so much of modern life for adults. Is it any wonder that today's adolescents —shorn from sturdy preindustrial social forms, adrift in a society that does not fulfill an adult's need for higher meaning—are ambivalent about gaining adult status?

How many times do adolescents hear their parents complain about their lives and their jobs? It is the fortunate adult indeed whose career meets not only his material needs but his emotional and spiritual ones as well.

Martin is one of the lucky ones. He is a biochemist whose research over the years has yielded important medical advances. Though now in his middle forties, Martin had always found science infinitely fascinating. From as far back as he could remember he had dreamed of becoming a scientist. For him it had an almost religious meaning. As a college student his models were professors whom he saw as passionately and disinterestedly immersed in the pursuit of truth. He also greatly admired men like Jonas Salk. Our society holds men like Salk in the highest esteem.

In short, Martin has been able to live out a life to which both he and society attach the highest meaning and value. As it turns out, his son John, now in college, is intending to follow in his father's footsteps. He shares his father's love of science and research. He also greatly admires his father's work. John, in other words, has a meaningful role to idealize and live up to (i.e., scientist). He also has a parent who embodies all those positive qualities he wants to emulate. Who he came from, what he is made of, what he wants to be, and the value of his vocation are all fused together.

Contrast this father and son with Harold and Rob. Harold has worked as a claims adjuster in a branch insurance office for the past twenty years. He finds the work neither meaningful nor gratifying. He has done it solely to make a living to support his family. To a degree, he also feels embittered. He knows society does not consider his work indispensable. It is not highly esteemed.

His son Rob likes him. But Rob, in contrast to John, is enormously conflicted about what he is going to do with his life. Why? On an unconscious level a child's self-esteem is heavily influenced by what he thinks of his parents. It poses itself in the mind thusly: "I come from my parents; therefore, whatever they are, I inherit. I consist of what they consist of. If they are unique, gifted, special people, so am I. If they are mediocre, third rate, then so am I."

The idea of following in his father's "philosophical" footsteps is intolerable to Rob. Seeing the rest of his life as drudging out a living makes him question whether he wants to go through with the rest of his adult life at all. Yet something he conceals shamefully inside tells him that since his father is only a claims adjuster, what could he possibly become?

American adolescents of today often seek a reason to live in order to help them answer the question, Who am I? A society with clear-cut roles that it invests with spiritual value, meaning, and importance can readily supply an adolescent with a reason to live. Do American society and American culture provide these things?

For the most part, no. It is a commercial culture geared toward maximum economic prosperity. Its values stress material acquisition and physical well-being. These inevitably come at the expense of spiritual values.

American mass culture is a commercial culture. It tries to maximize profits through products designed to appeal to the widest possible audience. In practice, this means products that seek the lowest common denominator. Often they are trivial, inane, and tasteless. Mass culture, and the homogenized, standardized life-styles it affords us, in major ways obliterates our individuality. It also intentionally obliterates the complexity, the harshness, and the depth of human life.

On one level that means that all of us must put up with an outrageously falsified sense of life and beauty. How accurate a picture of our culture would an anthropologist of the twenty-fourth century have were he to base his conclusions on a time capsule containing (and these are simply the items that spring immediately to mind) a "Dick Van Dyke Show" rerun, a copy of *Reader's Digest,* a brochure of Disney World, some bumper stickers reading "I Brake for Animals" and "I Found It," and a few postcards embossed with pictures of Denny's fast-food emporiums.

Whether mass culture, by definition, must be like this is another question. The point is that these things are, in their own ways, intellectually and aesthetically idiotic. They do not portray the risks, the conflicts, the nuances, which is to say the substance, of how we live or what we as Americans or human beings are like. No more than, say, the great block of seventeenth-century "sentimental" novels suggest the full dimension of life in that era.

Nevertheless, our culture pervades our daily lives, and we all, to one degree or another, partake of it. An American adolescent, however, normally undergoes an intellectual and aesthetic awakening. Just as he becomes more physically capable, he becomes more intellectually and critically aware. He is on the threshold entering "the adult world." Not only does he hope it will judge him approvingly, but he is and must be in a position to judge society as well. After all, is it not only sensible and human to evaluate a group, whether it be society, a corporation, a professional society, or a social club, before deciding if membership is worthwhile?

As a result many adolescents are overwhelmed with disillusionment. Adults know the world is abundantly stocked with inanities, greed, and hypocrisy. As adults we know that we have little choice but to live in the world as best we can without trying to make it over or totally abandoning our sense of integrity. There are, perhaps, parents who may openly display and even encourage certain kinds of dishonesty, such as infidelity and tax evasion, but they are in the minority.

Adolescents, however, normally need to envision the adult world, the world they are soon going to enter, as a safe and good place. In order to look forward to inhabiting one's place in the world one usually needs to see it as honest, just, and exciting. They may not feel they would be able to cope in any other kind of atmosphere. If the chaos within them is matched by an even greater chaos all around them, it can appear overwhelming and terrifying.

To a degree this is also true of the superficialities and the triviality they perceive. The disappointment and the despair they experience can also be overwhelming. This somewhat explains why adolescents so often try the understanding of their teachers and parents with their vociferous contempt of the world, the mercurial rages and depressions they express over trivial events or bits of mass culture. A "Charlie's Angels" show may spark an incendiary polemic on "truth and beauty" because life is not meeting an adolescent's need for a world that lives up to the standards inculcated when he was younger. It does not provide a structure of all-wise, all-fair, all-profound institutions, which are, in a tangible way, a derivation of how adolescents usually want to see their parents when very young. Because of an adolescent's insecurities and sense of smallness he wants the world to provide a reassuring polar opposite. That is one reason, incidentally, why adolescents so often see matters in black and white. They need absolute concepts, and project those expectations onto the world, to give them anchors for their raging uncertainties and insecurities.

If the world appears to be such a ridiculous, inane, and above all such a formless place, is it any wonder that so many adolescents are overwhelmingly confused and disoriented, unable for the life of them to find any self-respecting, meaningful, comfortable niche, let alone one designed to suit their particular personality? Where can they find some solid role to emulate, to pattern their own imminent adult lives after?

This is coupled with another major disillusionment, an even more threatening one, which revolves around one's parents. For we must remember that in a child's mind adults not only represent the larger world. They also embody its substance. From a child's perspective, which is all adolescents have known up until this stage, adults have absolute control over the world that they structure and administer at their discretion. This is not as astonishing as it might at first sound. As a small, dependent, helpless person a young child needs to see his parents this way. It is how the household is ordered. In order to feel protected from the larger world it is very comforting to feel one's parents are in charge on the outside as well.

Needless to say, it is also very comforting to feel that our parents are unique, all-powerful people because their strength provides us with the security and ability to choose our own destiny.

So, at first, the amorphousness of our mass culture and the crass drudgery of so many of the jobs in the world upset a major, perhaps indispensable, prop for an adolescent's sense of well-being. What usually takes place next, sometimes simultaneously, is the reevaluation of one's parents. On the one hand they still seem to be in control of the world, while on the other they no longer live up to that earlier, very precious, and painfully obsolete picture. A mother and father often try to instill values in a child. A person should be unstintingly honest, unreservedly courageous and outspoken, capable of undying selflessness in service to worthy causes, altruistic, hard working, loyal, kind, vibrant among others.

Who in real life is this marching band of virtues? An adolescent now has the embryonic equivalent of an adult's eyes in his head. He sees, for the first time, that his parents do not live up to the idealized picture he once formed. Suddenly he notices, perhaps, that the furniture he has grown up with is shabby and gaudy. His parents apparently are limited; they do not have an innate sense of taste.

He sees that physically they are flawed. They are run down, to some degree paunchy or sagging with age. Their conversation does not consist of profound and sensitive insights and pronouncements. It is largely a hodgepodge of small talk, dull gossip, prejudices, and the mundane routine matters of daily life.

Rather than working at noble, awe-inspiring endeavors their jobs are uninspiring, limited, unimaginative, and normally nothing the whole world looks up to and cannot live without. In our society, people are judged, by all but the most sophisticated, by what they do. It is a fact of life that some people have low-prestige jobs, others have bland ones, and still others make a great deal of money at vocations that could not be considered altruistic by any stretch of the imagination.

They indulge in mass culture during their leisure hours. They are not helping the poor or leading a charity drive, reading great literature or churning out masterpieces in oil in the attic.

They are exhausted and often irritable at the end of the long day, fitfully attempting to relax by reading the paper or *Reader's Digest,* bowling, or sitting listlessly in front of a television set.

In short, everything adolescents' parents taught them to be, and which they very much want to live up to, finds no counterpart in a world shorn of meaningful models. This perhaps would not be so totally devastating if their parents themselves stood apart as the immaculate shining exception to the rule. Far from being noble warriors, they are, suddenly, ordinary drones.

We shall have more to say later on about parents who

inadvertently have an actively destructive effect on their adolescents. Disillusionment leaves many adolescents, some suicidal, with the feeling of having been betrayed and reacting
toward reality with complete and bitter disappointment.
The end result is that they can find no one in the adult
world who can understand or appreciate them or provide
them with absolute answers.

Matters are routinely aggravated by the conflicts parents
and children have that arise over their different, if not mu-
tually exclusive, perspectives of the world. Adults who have
successfully struggled through life, which by the time they
have adolescent age children is usually the case, know that
for their children to be secure and comfortable they must
earn a good solid living.

Part of providing for one's children, on an emotional level,
is making certain they are ultimately free from the anxie-
ties of expenses, that they are independent and self-reliant.
Adults, therefore, think in practical terms, and so often the
most practical jobs are those whose primary, and perhaps
sole, function and gratification is making money. Schopenhauer's mercantile firm is a good example, one that, from
a parent's point of view, is reassuring. It fulfills his idea of
what a good, which is to say secure, life must be.

An adolescent measures the world, as we have seen, by
very different yardsticks. His needs are different. He also,
one must remember, has in all probability grown up hearing a litany of what feels like criticism from his parents.
Pick up your clothes, wash your face, straighten your room,
write those thank-you notes.

All these things in their own way are necessary for training a child to fit into the larger world. Still, many children
have grown up hearing stern and exasperated tones of
voice. If an adolescent is himself unsure about what he is
going to be, if he is on some level ashamed of and impa-
tient with his own confusion, he feels terribly vulnerable.
Under those conditions a parent's inquiry into his future

plans can feel like a loveless criticism, or an unbearable
pressure.

Sometimes, when a parent makes a suggestion that is at
polar opposites to what an adolescent secretly wants to be
encouraged to do, the suggestion itself can feel like a crushing rejection of his ambitions.

With all this in mind, it should come as no surprise that
today's adolescent often feels he has no one either inside
or outside his immediate environment who serves as an im-
movable pillar of certitude and support and understanding.
The utterly profound feelings of helplessness, vulnerability,
and alienation these factors combine to produce, as the statistics tell us, can be disastrous.

One must also remember that, whether or not this country's founding statesmen envisioned it just this way, our
society is a competitive one. That is the nature of a cap-
italist society: survival of the fittest, the shrewdest, the luckiest, and perhaps in practice the most ruthless.

At a time, then, when an adolescent is most in need of
support, he is suddenly thrust into a society—and school may
serve as a good example—that cannot help but be a mirror
of the culture that spawned it. Children may or may not be
initiated into the realms of art, history, and science. Still
schools function, if their charters are to be believed, to
prepare children for the larger world.

That means competition, competing for grades, competing
for approval and attention, competing for a place of prestige
in some organized extracurricular activity. We generally pay
lip service to this setup as simply an organized forum for the
cultivation of an individual's abilities and interests. In reality, adolescents are evaluated and judged against their fellow
classmates (who falls where on the grade curve and where
does that leave me?) two to three times every nine months.
And this occurs during the years in which a child is involved
in a constant back-and-forth match-up between what he
thinks of himself and what the world thinks of him.

A public relations executive with considerable experience and an impressive record of successful accounts can sooner or later take risks that do not pay off and survive the arbitrary withdrawal of accounts without being disturbed or feeling he is incompetent. Still, to some extent, each loss and failure leads to some painful feelings.

An adolescent who does not have a record of successful encounters is overcome by intense feelings of inadequacy. Whatever secret doubts he has about his ability to compete successfully—and how can he not have them when he has yet to prove himself in the adult world?—are exacerbated when he faces what appear to be such profoundly symbolic failures as might occur academically or in competitive sports. School provides a child with an environment in which he can compete before involving himself in the struggle for survival of adulthood.

Just as a child brings the lessons of his early infancy to meet adult situations, so too does he draw very serious conclusions from his successes and failures in competing with school chums.

In some ways it is positively amazing that so many adolescents do manage to survive adolescence, leaving the scars they have endured to be removed somehow with successes they encounter later on with a job or with the opposite sex.

Everybody needs to feel unique. Each of us develops a delight in our own unique and separate being at a very early age (no matter how much this feeling is challenged later on). As our parents told us, in a soothing voice when we were young: "You're a very special person and there is no one like you in the world."

To establish an adult identity also means finding our unique parts. We all need to feel that we are important, unreplicable beings with a special destiny, that we are distinguishable from the common mass.

Adolescents have to develop this conviction of uniqueness and definition of the self. This is an important goal of this stage of life. They need to feel that there is no one else like them. Instead, they are often plagued with the horrifying conviction that they are inadequate to cope with a complex world that accentuates their anxiety, shame, and weakness.

In a world in which only the strong survive, that horror is routinely magnified into devastating proportions. It is, in short, quite a bit removed from the communal supportive worlds of Montefegatesi and the Great Plains of the early nineteenth century.

Up until now I have not given many examples of adolescents who have succumbed to the strains I have outlined above. So, after providing some illustration, we can conclude with an examination of a phenomenon that has arisen among adolescents along with the rise in suicides. That is, cults, which claim an alarming number of adolescent adherents yearly. Some psychiatrists maintain, and I think accurately, that for many, cults represent a last-ditch effort to cope with conflicts that would otherwise drive these adolescents to suicide. At the very least, as we shall see, the cults themselves serve to illustrate how deeply an adolescent's need for a stable and supportive environment truly is.

For now, let us examine the problems confronting John and Judy.

John was a sixteen-year-old suburban youth who had always idolized his father. Ever since he could remember, John had admired him more than anyone else in the world. In John's eyes, his father was the most self-assured, the most forceful, kindest, most supportive, most successful person imaginable.

Not only was their day-to-day relationship a warm and close one, but John's father indulged the pleasure John took in him in every possible way. As an unusually prosperous businessman, he had more than adequate means at his disposal to do so. Virtually without exception, John had only to ask for something in order for it to be his.

The crowning gift, though, was probably the Mercedes-Benz sports coupe John received as a sixteenth-birthday present. If such a gift might be more than some adolescents would be prepared to handle comfortably, John took great pleasure in it, not so much for the elegance of the machine itself, although he enjoyed that, but in that it came from his father.

His feelings about it began to change, however. Or more accurately, he began to feel a vague boredom and dissatisfaction with it around the time he learned that his father derived most of his income from slum landlording, the occupation that had given him his start twenty years earlier. Prior to then, John had only the vaguest notion of how his father earned his living, and in any event he did not have the moral perspective he had begun to evolve as an adolescent.

Over a period of weeks, John began to use the car less and less frequently, finally leaving it in the garage altogether, preferring to walk, bicycle, or rely upon rides from friends. He eventually felt ashamed and indifferent to it. What was worse, John suddenly lost all interest in school. He stopped spending time with his buddies and found he no longer had any enthusiasm for joining his classmates at their weekly parties. He could not explain it, but he just did not have the nerve to show his face among them anymore.

He spent more and more time alone, off in a cloud, depressed, listless, and withdrawn. Without knowing why, he found himself wishing that he were dead. His depression and withdrawal acted like a vicious circle, and ultimately he drank a poisonous household substance in an attempt to end his life.

After this, he entered treatment with me. He could not make sense of his own feelings. He did not understand why he had suddenly become unhappy, only that within the recent past he had been seized with a desire to die. The sequence of events sketched above, the cause and effect, was something we were only able to piece together jointly after a long series of analytic sessions in which his father was the main topic of discussion.

At the root of John's problem was that the man he had looked up to more than anyone in the world had turned out to be an enormous disappointment. Slum landlording is by no means an illegal profession. John's father, in fact, enjoyed a great deal of prestige in his community and served admirably on a number of civic and community boards.

To John, his father's occupation was a morally repulsive one, and therefore the prestige his father received, from both his son and his community, seemed undeserved. His father, in short, had become a fake, a liar, someone who sucked the lifeblood from the poor. Everything connected with his father, which in the past had been savored on the basis of admiration and trust, seemed worthless. John felt that if the man he loved most had perpetrated a massive betrayal on him, then the world itself could not be trusted. Life itself, therefore, was not worth pursuing.

The fact that John did not see all this clearly from the outset should not be surprising. Suppose, for example, on some level an employee knows that his position in his company is quietly slipping or perhaps that his marriage is facing major difficulties. Problems like these are ones most people would prefer to disappear. Facing them can be too threatening, as though it would amount to inviting them to happen. Therefore one often deals with problems by putting them out of one's mind and telling oneself what one would like to believe: Nothing is wrong. Since almost no adolescent, or adult for that matter, is so introspective as to comprehend the innermost working of his mind, a feeling of disappointment this subtle and this massive would usually escape conscious scrutiny. For if he had been able to admit his feelings openly, the overwhelming, frightening rage and sense of loss he felt toward his father would also have had to come out. The intensity of this kind of rage is often too disruptive to deal with openly.

When the primary source of goodness, support, and hope in John's environment disappeared, he felt crushed and forsaken, a feeling that in a different way Judy also encountered.

Judy came from a loving but troubled household. Her father was a physician whose cold, detached manner made him an ideal clinician but a withdrawn and unsympathetic father. Like many dedicated physicians. he spent many of his evenings at the hospital where he chaired a department.

Judy's mother was a kind soul but a somewhat frantic one. She depended upon her husband to make all decisions, not only in financial and household matters but in her own life. She also tended to lean upon amphetamines and alcohol. She was well intentioned but insecure and self-involved. Both Judy's parents were in their early sixties when she turned fifteen.

For all these reasons Judy got along poorly with her parents. Not only did they not understand her, but they were largely unavailable to her emotionally whether or not she was trying to solve an adolescent crisis.

Judy was also an early bloomer, physically, and resembled a stunning blond starlet by the time she was a sophomore. At the time she did not feel like a starlet, but an alienated, frightened fifteen-year-old, someone who desperately needed a strong, warm source of adult involvement.

This she found in her high school English teacher, a person in his late twenties, who combined a charismatic manner and a love of literature with a flair for poetry, which he occasionally indulged by reading his latest inspiration in class.

Judy was enthralled. She could not put it into words, but here was someone who seemed to be a dream come true. His rumpled hair, thick moustache, and casual, unorthodox dress fit her ideal of the sensitive, searching, ethereal poet, someone totally unlike anyone else she had ever met. He seemed to know so many esoteric, lovely things and saw into the human heart, in her eyes, far better than any of the other adolescents or faculty members around her.

From the first she began to linger after class waiting for the other students to leave simply to .be around him, to struggle for something to say to him, to laugh and giggle when he responded with a kind and disarming remark. Soon she found herself staunchly defending whatever he said in class, and following that up with ever more lengthy post-class discussions, which eventually became more confessional and revealing.

She had, in short, built the teacher into everything she wanted and needed in a parent and older brother. The teacher did not quite know how to handle her attention. He had never had so beautiful a girl "fall at his feet" before, and being immature, he slowly found himself wanting to see her admiration in a romantic light. He knew, of course, that he was not really the demigod she had built him into. But slowly and surely he made the transition from detachment to feeling flattered to a very strong and very covert infatuation.

Judy, without realizing it, had been desperately in need of a person who could supply, at a safe and appropriate distance, the emotional supports she did not have at home. Feelings she was not comfortable enough to feel openly toward her father she could feel toward her teacher. This is by no means an unusual occurrence. In fact, it is routine among adolescents and is one reason, for example, why boys at this stage often enter into an intensely confessional relationship with a sympathetic aunt. It is much easier, in an adolescent's mind, to find a strong, sympathetic authority figure to depend upon outside one's immediate family than it is to form an equivalent relationship with a member of the family upon whom he is totally dependent.

As we shall see in a subsequent chapter, an adolescent of-

ten tries to rebel against such a family member to help
create his own independent identity.

Just as Judy would have been traumatized had her father
made an open sexual advance upon her, so did she find herself thrown into enormous turmoil when her English teacher
attempted to make love to her during what had become one
of innumerable after-hours private conferences in his office.

The teacher, of course, had committed a highly unethical
offense. Rather than stepping back and trying to understand what Judy's true needs were and using his influence
with her to direct her toward counseling or therapy, he
encouraged and exacerbated her dependency to the breaking point.

The end result was that Judy came away from that evening with mounting headaches. She woke up screaming in
the middle of the night, dreaming that an ax was about to
split her skull. For several days thereafter she was unable to
attend her English class, so overwhelmed was she with guilt
and shame for "what she had done." The image of the ax
falling onto her skull seemed to crowd out all other thoughts.

She walked the halls in a daze, unable to retain her attention long enough to conduct the most cursory conversation.
Within two weeks she was accidentally injured by a car when
she stepped into the middle of the street, her mind in a
fog.

In both John's and Judy's cases their environments had
removed the stability and the supports they needed to work
out their emotional conflicts. Society itself had, as we have
previously outlined, failed to provide them with a comfortable niche. When members of their immediate group
also failed them, the combination proved too much to handle. From an emotional point of view they were in the
position of a cartoon character who flees off the edge of
a cliff, notices in midair that there is nothing underneath
him, and then plummets earthward.

Cults, such as those who once followed Rev. Jim Jones

and those who today worship the Reverend Moon (Moonies, as they are called), have reacted to the amorphousness of the real world around them by retreating into a self-contained and insulated world. When a person fundamentally does not know the answers, perhaps not even the questions, then only a system that knows them all will work. Cults thrive among those who need to believe in an omnipotent provider.

A group like this has a cohesiveness and a unanimity unknown in the real world, which can be enormously reassuring to those desperate to escape their raging uncertainties. The need can be so strong that they, the cultists, reject the world's reality for that of the group. An adolescent who seeks escape from normal adult authority finds just the sanctuary he needs in a cult, which has the added advantage of being anathema to most working people, who are totally excluded from it.

The cult supplies its members with an absolute reason to live. Sadly enough, it is just these adolescents, who so obviously need strong support, who evoke such angry and bitter reactions from most adults. It's hardly unusual, for example, to see a businessman confronted by the beatific, serene-looking Hari Krishna member at an airport react in a violent manner. The idea that the Krishnas have found the absolute ideal solution to life infuriates most of us. The fact that these cultists assume a smug and condescending manner toward the uninitiated is also routinely misinterpreted.

For we must keep in mind that someone who is truly comfortable in his or her beliefs normally does not find it necessary to regard others as unredeemed if they happen to believe differently. There is no more staunch and enthusiastic champion of Catholicism than Pope John Paul II. Although he is in some sense the very embodiment of his faith on earth, his presence affects people in a much different, much warmer way. People of all faiths can enjoy and admire him, even though Catholicism is a proselytizing faith.

Beneath the surface of John Paul's comfort with his beliefs is a self-evident certainty, while very near the surface of a cultist's arrogant self-assurance are tremendous insecurities.

The reality of the Moonie, by contrast to the pope's, is shared and limited to a relatively small group of people who undoubtedly have many similar personal needs.

Whether the subgroup to which an adolescent adheres is religious, political, or artistic, all claim superiority over the rest of society. It is almost as if the members, having deep reservations about their own adequacy, find a club for themselves that will turn the tables on the society that threatens them—making it "inferior" instead. These groups do not, I beg you to notice, normally produce works of any lasting humanitarian or artistic value (movements such as the Abstract Expressionists and Impressionists were not composed of adolescents and constitute a whole different category).

The boundless self-confidence they display, therefore, is betrayed by the impotence they bring to the possibility of concrete contributions to society.

None of this is to say that all adolescents who form subgroups are carriers of severe emotional illness. In some cases these groups serve a very important purpose, which we shall be discussing in chapter 4.

What is important here is that adolescents find a pervasive sense of "calm" within cults, which ultimately proves inadequate and illusory. It works as a vehicle to contain the chaos these youngsters feel. When their environment only intensifies their sense of aimlessness, they simply create a unique ideology and an alternative life-style. That is their solution. Their system is based upon illusions.

But what else do they have? They do not know how to live. This is a problem that confronts many other adolescents who are actively engaged in trying somehow to find a place for themselves in the mainstream of our society. It is to the most common conflicts and destructive environments they encounter that we must now turn.

PART TWO

How Do We Live?

It will generally be found that when the terrors
of life outweigh the terrors of death
a man will put an end to his life.

ARTHUR SCHOPENHAUER

CHAPTER 4

Why Is Living So Difficult?

W<small>E HAVE OBSERVED</small> somewhat earlier that adolescence is a transitional period in which one's identity is in a constant state of change and therefore of uncertainty. In fact, adolescents occupy a position roughly analogous to that of immigrants huddled on a steamer slowly making its way to the New World. The immigrants on that boat, having forfeited the world they knew, were in transit to a new life that they could not realistically visualize. Standing on neither shore they inhabited a netherworld all their own.

The majority of adolescents occupy a type of limbo. Their childhoods are slowly receding behind them while they move slowly and inexorably to the unknown continent of adulthood. In our society they are neither full-fledged children nor full-fledged adults. Both those worlds, and the identities they provide, are out of reach and beyond their grasp. So perhaps it is no wonder that they tend to form a subworld all their own, a world that excludes those much younger and much older, a world they are simultaneously driven to and create voluntarily.

What are the major features of this subworld? What are the major traumas they will inevitably face within it? What positive and indispensable functions does it serve? How does it break down and sometimes destroy its members? How does adolescence itself all but compel a son or daughter to respond to the adult world—to use adults in order to form their own identity?

Up until now we have been examining adolescence, and the reasons that underlie the rising suicide rate among them, from the banks of two different shores, the old world of childhood and the new world of adulthood. We have looked at how an adolescent perceives adults and outlined the problems he confronts in attempting to find a place within their world. We have also explored the basis of the earliest forces that help to determine how an adolescent may cope with life.

The question, Who am I? is perhaps the major one adolescents wrestle with. It is followed very closely by the struggle to create an independent identity. This is one reason adolescents "band together." To the outsider, attending a national convention of housewares manufacturers would probably be a terrible bore. Outsiders do not share the very special problems, ambitions, and concerns of that group. The manufacturers, on the other hand, deal with these things on an intimate, day-to-day basis. They are the only ones who can "understand" their common difficulties. They are the only ones who can share this major element of their professional lives.

The intensity with which adolescents band together is much greater than that which unites businessmen. Adolescents depend upon their subworld to help them create a new and durable identity.

This is not done in total isolation from the adult world. The mother is crucial to her child's ultimate ability to survive. By this, I hasten to add, I mean neither to single out mothers (fathers also play an important role) nor to imply that absolutely everything depends upon a mother's ability to deliver an overabundance of never ending emotional support.

Emotional support is crucial, and its long-standing absence can be fatal. Just as important are the adolescent's conscious and unconscious feelings and strong reactions to what he perceives his parents to be. They may be an accurate reflection, or they may not. The crucial fact is that if an adolescent believes a parent is an omnipotent, vengeful ogre, then consequently he would rather end his life than face his father's wrath over a disciplinary problem in high school. The gap between imagination and reality is nonexistent for all practical purposes. For if an adolescent has a belief, and acts upon it, it amounts to the same thing.

This is a major reason why the struggle for an independent identity often ends in suicide. An adolescent, we must remember, is struggling to bring three worlds into synchrony, those of childhood, adolescence, and adulthood. Most adults routinely encounter major problems and stresses simply carrying on with the identity they have. So it should not be surprising that someone juggling three might lose control.

We will then of necessity also devote pages within this section to two lamentable problems, problems that are not commonly discussed in the general literature. I am referring to destructive parenting and those conflicts, similar to those of Ross Lockridge's, that beset many suicidal adolescents. A bit later I will describe some of the most common symptoms and warning signs of an impending suicide attempt. For all of this, the earlier discussions will provide us with a background.

At this juncture, though, a discussion of the major features and traumas of the adolescent subworld is important.

If asked to name the generation of adolescents who constituted the most striking subgroup in recent memory, most people would probably point to those young people who grew up in the late sixties and early seventies. They were the ones who were coming of age during the greatest national internal upheavals since the Great Depression. Part of their visibility was due to their sheer numbers. They were the offspring of the postwar baby boom. One could say they emerged out of the unobtrusive quiet preadolescence years into a mass adolescence that nearly swamped the physical capacities of our nation's college campuses.

Anyone who has raised a child just entering adolescence knows what change occurs in the household when that happens. Anyone who has raised twins knows how much more disruptive that can be than raising just one child. Viewing America for the moment as one enormous family in which the parents are suddenly swamped with a bursting household of adolescents, it is no wonder they made such an impact.

Their visibility was also due to the fortuitous emergence of the civil rights movement, the women's rights movement, and the Vietnam war. I say fortuitous because these upheavals in which these adolescents were so often active and effective participants coincided with needs they would have had to channel anyway, the need to rebel and the need to be a part of altruistic causes.

The outward and the secret features of this generation are worth examining. For their themes, in one form or another, are echoed (if less rambunctiously) by today's adolescents. That past adolescent generation, not incidentally, also left a series of vivid impressions familiar to us all and therefore especially handy for discussion.

Like most adolescents, this generation felt very keenly, much more keenly than adults or children, the age span they occupied. There is no better proof of just how strongly it affected them than their dictum "Don't trust anybody over thirty."

For here we have something no one has any control over, something entirely arbitrary, and something that is the very soul of ephemerality. Age, for all the importance it has for our emotional development (though age is by no means synonymous with wisdom and maturity), for all the responsibilities that come with it, is not a viable life principle equivalent to, for example, Marxist doctrine or biblical teachings.

Yet here was a group who raised age difference to the level of an ideology. There is hardly a clearer example to be found of a group taking what they feel to be their own inadequacies and their own feelings of uselessness and turning them into incomparable assets that they and they alone possess. One must remember that the age equation was propounded with what seemed to all the world like an inviolable smugness and superiority.

This is not to say that their political impact was not generally highly positive. Segregation, gratuitous wars, presidential subversion of individual liberties, and hopelessly hypocritical and demoralizing sexual codes were each in varying degrees festering national sores. We are well rid of them, let us hope.

Still, anyone who is the least familiar with the history of mankind and the innumerable societies he created knows that the corruption that this generation bewailed as the worst ever was nothing of the kind. The generation itself, experiencing disillusion on a mass scale for the first time, reacted to it as if it were the ultimate catastrophe. In fact, and this is in no way a defense of corruption, it was hardly at the same level of that of Imperial Rome (which depended upon slavery and imperialism), fourteenth-century Spain, Nazi Germany, South Africa, and so on.

Our purpose here is not to criticize a generation, but to see how its behavior and attitudes, when stripped to their essentials, can teach us something about adolescence today and the factors that drive some children to suicide.

This generation, as probably all generations of adolescents, was operating from motives of which they were scarcely aware, simply because they were too threatening and painful to face at the time.

This group, for example, evolved a whole series of values that fell under the catch-all phrase of "the counterculture." In banding together to form their own world, insulating themselves from the vast adult one that frightened them (with good reason), they claimed to reject everything. If that were truly the case, however, why is the counterculture today little more than a cultural fossil or relic? Would anyone seriously contend that this generation made good on their insistence that they would refuse to participate in our consumer-competitive-conformist culture? Are these millions of relatively young adults today spirited away in communes, dedicated to subsistence farming, growing their hair down to their shoulders, and reveling in the splendors of marijuana, LSD, and Ravi Shankar?

Of course not. They are today the up-and-coming lawyers, doctors, accountants, and condo converters. In a growing number of cases, both young men and women have decided to pursue professional careers and enjoy a relatively luxurious standard of consumer-style living through their joint incomes.

If the uproar they created had no lasting value but an ephemeral one, if their ideology was not in the last analysis to be taken at face value, what was its true purpose? How does it carry over into our understanding of today's adolescents?

We have already touched upon one important ingredient, that is, dealing with one's own vulnerabilities by turning them into strengths and making the outside world the one that is useless, irrelevant, inadequate, disappointing, unacceptable, insensitive, and ignorant.

Their revolt was really, in one sense, only a reaction to the enormous pressures to become competent adults, pressures these adolescents were not at the time prepared to handle smoothly.

Adults tend to view college as an idyllic, pressure-free environment in which children spend as much of their parents' money as they possibly can, dropping them a note only when the funds are running a little short, and devoting their spare time to hedonistic, guilt-free indulgence.

By and large, however, this is not the case. Adults tend to

envy adolescents their youth, their freedom from mundane jobs, and their inconsistency in decrying adults while living off their largess.

This image of the adolescent is largely the creation, one is tempted to say the illusion, of adults themselves. It normally bears very little relation to how adolescents live and it certainly is counterproductive to any accurate understanding of their dilemma.

One colleague of mine once observed that the adolescents really to be concerned about (that is, the most troubled) are the ones who act as though everything is just fine. He did not mean that there are not a few extraordinarily secure and well-adjusted adolescents, but rather that it is much more common to find adolescents who are so overwhelmed by the problems confronting them that they block them out, refusing to admit them to themselves.

No matter how brave and eager a face most adolescents put on, their impending departure from home and hearth for the beginning of their freshman year in college is often a highly disturbing event.

It is, in most cases, the first time they have been away from home for a long period. In fact, it has much more symbolic significance. It is the first day of the rest of one's life. Anyone who enlisted in the military service at eighteen, hoping for adventure, to be a man, to escape a destructive home life, can probably well recall the terror that, to some degree, besets most adolescents who have reached college age. That first night, when the recruit or enlistee is bedding down in the barracks, is not so very different from that first night when the family car recedes from sight and an adolescent is somewhere in a huge darkened dormitory filled with people and institutions entirely foreign to him. The unavoidable question is, Can I make it on my own? The natural fear is of failure, of being in the end too insecure and incompetent to leave the family nest, of returning home disgraced and overwhelmed by homesickness. For the old, presumably supportive, environment has become physically unavailable. How to find another?

Most adolescents go off to school not knowing who they are, not knowing what they are supposed to do with their lives, not knowing what their innate talents are or how to use them productively, not knowing even if society will permit them to be used as they please (how many people who entered college dreaming of becoming novelists never came closer than ad copywriting?).

Rather than being an idyllic setting, the college atmosphere is an extremely high-pressured one, if not academically, then certainly emotionally, though the two different sources of pressure generally occur simultaneously.

The sixties generation's rejection of the adult conformist-commercial society (which adults themselves have mixed feelings about) was in great measure a desperate attempt to slow down the maddening tempo of a highly competitive, materialistically oriented environment.

It is indeed ironic that adults tend to view a teeming college campus as one homogeneous mass while in fact its individual members are struggling to establish the various parts of their identities one by one. Am I feminine? Am I a real man? Am I academically gifted? Do I match up with my surroundings? These are all different parts of what will, with a lot of anguish and hard work, one day be a cohesive, consistent identity.

Not all college freshmen are up to this enormous task. Erik Erikson described those who cannot cope with this strain as people suffering from an "identity diffusion syndrome." In plain words, this means simply that they cannot effectively bring all the different facets of who they are and who they are striving to be into synchrony.

The problem is most frequently seen among college freshmen away from home for the first time. These are the youngsters who simply cannot shift smoothly from one role to another, from one way of spending their time to another.

They simply cannot smoothly move from being a student to a social companion to a political activist or to a lover. Each role seems foreign and clumsy to them and they often experience it with overwhelming bewilderment, confusion, and a painful awareness of how incongruous their surroundings seem. They cannot compose an organized picture of themselves that fits with the world around them.

College freshmen can feel this deeply enough to be pushed into suicide. Ellen was an eighteen-year-old college freshman who had done better than average work in high school. She was popular, she participated in various extracurricular activities and, in general, seemed to be a happy, reasonable, well-adjusted student.

In college, which in her case happened to be a large Big Ten school, she initially seemed quite stable. She kept up with her studies and became part of a social group that spontaneously sprang up in the dormitory where she lived.

Things went well for a few weeks. Then her friends noticed that she had become distant. She stopped participating in the usual late-night pajama parties and gossip sessions. Instead she stayed in her room, sitting, doing nothing, and staring into space. Soon she stopped bathing, brushing her teeth, or changing her clothes. When spoken to she either mumbled some inaudible monosyllabic answer or simply did not respond.

At first her friends respected what they interpreted to be a need for privacy. They became concerned, however, when they saw the mounting mess her room had become. Finally they all but dragged her to the student health service, to which she put up no resistance.

After a two-day hospitalization, Ellen's parents came to visit. They offered to remove her and take her back home until she felt better. At this, the patient gradually began to become coherent and alive. Ellen decided to remain in school and work her problems through with a psychiatrist on a regular basis.

Through her visits, Ellen began to talk about her overwhelming confusion. She literally had no idea who she was. She appeared calm on the outside, but inside she was tormented with panic. In high school she was able to carry on, perhaps because she knew what it was like to be "a kid." When she was simply uprooted one day, placed in an entirely new setting, and told that from here on she was to be an adult, she became emotionally disoriented. Her old picture of herself had become invalidated in her own mind. She felt somehow that her new persona was something akin to an enormous jigsaw puzzle scattered over the floor. She had no clue, and could not justify to herself, how each piece fit together or what the whole puzzle was supposed to look like.

Ellen's predicament is common. She would have very likely committed suicide had her friends not intervened. The pace at which she was falling apart would have ultimately left her feeling that her life was a hopeless, worthless muddle. Eventually, devoid of self-respect, unable to tolerate the misery any longer, she would have had to "do something" about her life, about her confusion. Most likely her solution would have been to snuff her life out.

Fred, in contrast, did not isolate himself in his room. He too stopped taking care of his appearance as a result of his emotional problems. Nevertheless, he sought out friends constantly. He plagued them with innumerable frenzied questions. He asked incessantly whether life had any meaning, whether there was any purpose to his existence.

He looked perpetually harassed, and his tension was contagious. He made people around him nervous, and his anxiety, in his friends' eyes, bordered on panic. Finally, driven to find some kind of relief from his overwhelming agitation, Fred checked himself into the student health center, where he received tranquilizing drugs at his request.

Unlike Ellen, Fred had some idea of who he was but he could see himself in only one role at a time, which meant that he spent enormous amounts of energy trying to block out the other parts of his inner spectrum.

In Fred's particular case, he was the son of a wealthy southern industrialist, sent to school in a large, radical northern university. The values his new surroundings embraced—antimaterialistic, Marxist, affirmative action—challenged, at their very roots, the values in which he was raised.

Some people find the fundamental challenge to their old life-style and system of values the most stimulating and valuable part of their college experience. The opportunity to rethink their beliefs and attitudes is indispensable to a solid identity of one's choosing. People with pretentions to self-understanding and the capacity for intellectual achievement must be able to subject themselves and their ideas to such a process. How else can one separate and eliminate irrational prejudice from truth? Some philosophers, such as John Stuart Mill, consider the challenge one of the main purposes of a liberal education.

Some children, like Fred, come to college too vulnerable and too shaky to withstand the challenge. Fred never had a deep sense of self-confidence, and when he left home the tenuous emotional support he enjoyed was removed.

In his mind his southern background belonged to one part of his personality, his northern education to another. Instead of becoming integrated, they remained at odds with each other. Just before he was hospitalized, Fred began to act out in the real world the conflicts he felt within him. He found that he could not conduct a variety of activities in one confined space. He studied each subject on his curriculum inside a different campus building (i.e., physics in the physics building, English in the English building, etc.).

He socialized with his southern friends at one end of campus, violently objecting if they wanted to visit the place his northern friends frequented. Bizarre as this may sound, it fit perfectly with the nature of his turmoil. With some psychiatric help he too, like Ellen, recovered quickly and functioned normally, conducting his social and academic life much as his peers did.

Of course, these kinds of breakdowns are not simply restricted to one's freshman year. They can, and do, take place earlier. As a rule, people of all ages have to bring the way they see themselves into harmony with what the world thinks of them and how the world treats them.

I, for example, am a practicing psychoanalyst, a teacher, and a published author. Professionally, this is how I see myself, and the world is more or less willing to see me this way too. It grants me the appropriate titles, permits me to earn my living and build a professional reputation according to my capacities.

Were I to walk into Carnegie Hall tomorrow and insist that the management put out handbills advertising my intention of performing Franz Liszt's B-Minor Piano Sonata, they would politely show me to the door. This would not be a serious matter, perhaps, unless I did not see myself as a psychoanalyst at all, but a professional concert pianist. If I were so convinced of my pianistic identity that I held parties in which I sat my captive audience down to hear me play, if I did not let the Carnegie Hall matter drop, but instead introduced myself as a pianist and began trooping from concert hall to concert hall proclaiming my virtuosity, I would eventually be in store for some devastating blows to my self-esteem.

The world would implacably refuse to acknowledge or reinforce my sense of who I was.

However farfetched that example might seem, it illuminates an important point for understanding adolescents and the reasons behind some of their suicides.

As the rest of us, the way adolescents do things helps determine what they are and how they see themselves. People are considered realistic when their picture of themselves matches that of the world. When people are comfortable with that match they become content. When those two images do not match for an adolescent, he or she can feel tremendously isolated and alienated. That alienation can build to a peak that is ultimately unbearable.

So it was with Sally, a girl who took her own life before she was seventeen. As a child Sally was precocious, gifted, and strikingly attractive. She sang, danced, and acted, winning a great deal of adulation from her friends and her elders.

On the surface her childhood seemed idyllic. During adolescence all that changed. Like many adolescents who lose their little-girl charm and become gawky teenagers, Sally entered high school suddenly "demoted" to a very plain-looking child. Her singing voice turned out to be average, and her other qualities, which once drew so much admiration, withered away.

The loss of these talents, which she associated perhaps naturally enough with the reasons why people would love her, was so precipitous that she came to believe her former admirers were now either indifferent to her or openly contemptuous.

By the beginning of her sophomore year Sally was convinced that she was a hopeless and thorough failure as a human being.

Although she was not aware of it, she had never really felt secure and loved during childhood. She had thought of herself as someone who at the very least had to perpetually occupy a pedestal from which she received endless adoration. To keep it, she felt she had to pour out superhuman amounts of talent.

When the situation changed during adolescence, as it so often does with the overly doted-upon, she was devastated. It is understandable that she had carried her traditional view of herself into adolescence, but she could not cope with a world that abruptly stopped agreeing with her self-assessment.

She could not live up to the standards she now held herself accountable for. She was a plain, average girl and the harder she tried to make her unrealistic private reality fit, the more she thought herself to be a failure.

Finally she wrote a suicide note lamenting the disappointment she must have been for everybody, herself most of all.

It must be remembered that the subworld, the separate and distinct adolescent world into which people such as Sally enter, is probably no crueler, per se, than the adult one. Rather, the vast majority of people in it are infinitely more vulnerable. Since it is composed of people who are not secure, mature adults, the environment itself cannot be sufficiently supportive.

It is no coincidence that within any high school class a rigid and often destructive pecking order is established upon such transcendent values as good looks, good clothes, facile glib mannerisms, and whether one has a clear complexion or not. Snobbery is a way of making up for one's secret feelings of inferiority. Only people who are afraid they are not basically as good as the next person devote so much vituperative and cruel energy into asserting their superiority by making others feel inferior.

The tremendous emphasis teenagers so often place on who has and who lacks an abundance of these superficial qualities is really only a reflection of how threatened they feel by their own inadequacies in the face of the adult world. Adolescents who desperately want to be liked, to belong, to carve out an acceptable niche in their subworld are often simply practicing or trying out for the impending "big plunge" they must soon make into adulthood.

Since many adolescents enter the subworld with very little knowledge as to the kind of adults they will turn out to be, the wounds they encounter can take on a primal or prototypical importance. That is, "If I'm inadequate now it probably means I'm inadequate, period, and will run up against the same rejection and disappointment throughout my life."

Not long ago a free-lance writer published a very successful book composed of interviews with celebrities such as Henry Kissinger, who discussed how lonely, inadequate, and unpopular they felt in high school. They remembered these traumas in perfect detail thirty and forty years after they occurred. Some even went so far as to say that the ambition and drive that made them successes later were fueled in good measure by a hunger to overcome the deep wounds they felt, and to get back at the cheerleader or the football star who rejected their advances or ridiculed them in front of their peers.

Just as the lack of a stable, supportive environment in a person's early years can have a devastating impact later on, so can that same lack spell disaster when it occurs in the adolescent subworld.

Gary was a child prodigy who attended a small private high school in New England populated by the sons and daughters of college professors.

His father, a professor of chemistry, noticed that Gary was unusually adept at numbers almost from the moment he could walk. He taught Gary addition, subtraction, division, and fractions at the age of three and a half. Astounded by the ease with which his son mastered the material (he did not even seem to need his father's help except to give formal names to processes he already understood), his father taught Gary algebra by the time he was four. By the age of five, Gary had mastered geometry and before his seventh birthday he was an expert in differential calculus, thereby exhausting everything his father could teach him.

Before Gary had entered third grade he had already been interviewed by a panel of university mathematics professors and was scheduled for special after-school tutoring in advanced college-level studies. Surprisingly enough, his high school classmates did not, as most such groups probably would, ostracize him for being "freakish." Gary attended a school where intellectual achievements were valued by students and parents alike. Unlike some public high schools where students feel threatened by their inability to achieve and therefore shun those who are scholastically superior, Gary's peers went out of their way to help him cope.

Like many prodigies, Gary dressed sloppily, oblivious to the latest clothing styles. He was relatively short and stout and did not show much interest or initiative in getting dates with girls. Worst of all for his own welfare, Gary walked around in a mathematical cloud, so much so that he did not seem to hear the bell announcing the end of lunch period. He had trouble finding his way from one class to the next. His answers in math class were beyond even the teacher's ability to understand. His responses in all other classes were oblique and sometimes unintelligible.

Though a prodigy, Gary was also a human being like the rest of his peers. He was not inherently a math machine. On some level his massive preoccupation with the one thing he excelled at was fueled by a desperate effort to block out the raging inadequacies he felt in other areas. He was so afraid that he could not fit into other important aspects of adolescent and adult life that he retreated into his "math shell."

As long as Gary was in that special private high school with supportive students, he functioned well enough to get by. It was only when that environment was taken away from him that he fell apart. For when he entered a high-level New England university, his math shell was not enough. There were no people to shepherd him from class to class, from cafeteria to dormitory and other places. Before the first semester was over, Gary found himself unable to function altogether and sadly he was removed to a mental hospital, where he remains to this day.

One of the most common mistakes parents of floundering adolescents make is to confuse a stable and secure environment with a rigid, disciplined one. A parent may see a child become more and more slovenly, inattentive, careless about schoolwork, and perhaps prone to antisocial outbursts such as petty vandalism and vituperative confrontations with teachers. After a year or two of this, and it invariably comes as part of an overall pattern, parents may be so baffled and angry that they decide the only thing that will correct a son may be a military academy.

In a few cases, an environment of strict limits, narrow rules, and harshly enforced restrictions turns out to be helpful. In most instances, however, what appears to the parent to be a simple and straightforward solution does not get at the root of an adolescent's emotional difficulties. Instead, it has the effect of closing off an ear to the hidden wellsprings of the child's behavior and polarizes him and his environment to the breaking point.

Howard had all the above-mentioned difficulties and symptoms. He was an unusually gawky and clumsy teenager who had never done well at school, had no particular academic acumen, and, after repeated failures, stopped studying altogether.

He grew insolent and lazy at home, attended class infrequently, never doing, let alone turning in, the majority of his homework assignments. Uninterested in after-school activities, rejecting the increasingly few overtures for friendship he received, he became a self-centered loner. Finally, after smashing in a row of classroom windows one evening, he was picked up by the police and suspended from school.

In his self-rejection, Howard had taken out his rage against the institution that he, without knowing it, had manipulated into rejecting him. His father had no way of knowing how to interpret his son's behavior other than that it was deeply disturbing and a direct reflection on his own parenting.

Within the next three months, Howard found himself shipped off to a military academy in the Midwest to "straighten himself out." His father assumed that the academy would impose a discipline that Howard would, if not make his own, at least learn to conform to.

It had precisely the opposite effect. Although it was too painful to admit openly, Howard felt deeply inadequate and rejected by his father's decision. It seemed to Howard that he had not been terribly loved at home in the first place. Now he proved himself so unworthwhile that his family wanted him out of the house and out of the state. He was supposed to study, but what most filled his mind was an incoherent surge of terror and hatred.

Cut off from his home environment, he found himself at the mercy of an even more hostile adolescent subworld. In a milieu where sloppiness is cause for vituperative brow-beating and harassment, Howard soon found he was the favorite whipping boy of his upperclassmen. The antagonism toward him deepened when his peers began to poke around for chinks in Howard's armor, as they routinely did with each other as well. In Howard they found a gold mine.

Howard's delinquency, his toughness, was all façade. He was an unusually uncoordinated teenager and had neither the prowess nor the nerve to successfully stand up to what had become, to say the least, an unsupportive environment. His day-to-day life soon devolved into a series of tongue lashings, shunnings, work punishments, and beatings.

Finally he snapped. Late one night he broke into the armory, where he was discovered holding a rifle and searching desperately for the store of ammunition with which he could "blow his fucking head off" once and for all.

The contrast between Gary's classmates and Howard's is strikingly and painfully vivid. It is also worth underscoring if only because it contains a lesson for parents and teachers. That is, here we have two very different styles of dealing with an adolescent's overwhelming vulnerabilities. On some level, Gary's classmates recognized their own vulnerability, their own incompetence, in him. They were not threatened by their feelings. Their compassion, helpfulness, and em-pathy, although directed toward Gary, also helped to reassure themselves that their individual vulnerabilities could be handled with acceptance and understanding. The relation-ship they had to the outside world, to Gary, said something very healthy about their relationship to themselves.

Howard's peers also recognized their own weaknesses in him, although they may not have been consciously aware of it. They were so threatened by weakness that they did ev-erything they could to stamp it out, violently, in themselves. When they saw it in someone else, they directed their own private intolerance, fueled by fear, onto him. Certainly, Gary was a harmless instance of helplessness and did nothing to scare other people off (his "oddness" apart). Howard was more problematic. He had, in the past, rejected what seemed to everyone a helping hand.

These boys are extreme examples. Most adolescents are neither totally dependent upon a supportive subgroup to function nor pitted against an overwhelmingly hostile and destructive circle of peers. Most adolescents fall somewhere in the middle. At times they feel intensely close to and un-derstood by those around them. At other times they feel inadequate and humiliated by them. In any case adolescents invariably place enormous emotional importance upon find-ing a secure niche within their peer group and receiving crucial support and approval from it. As people who are neither adults nor children, adolescents often feel cut adrift. No longer able to cling to their parents as they once did, their peer group often takes on the importance of a life jacket buoying them up and keeping them afloat amid their uncertainties.

What usually makes each individual adolescent's plight so problematic is that the peer group to which he gravitates is, by definition, composed of members who are all relatively insecure. It would be unrealistic to expect the group to be anything other than what it invariably turns out to be, an inconsistent gathering that offers support and instability in virtually equal measure.

To better understand what this means for our nation of adolescents we shall return briefly to that highly visible generation who set themselves so vividly apart and gave us so many revealing glimpses into the true nature of this difficult period of life.

CHAPTER 5

Life Is Exciting but Painful

Somewhere between the adoption of unorthodox hair length and outlandish dress, the sixties generation came to be designated as "freaks." It is a very revealing nickname. The current generation of adolescents, though not nearly as flamboyant, share that feeling of "freakiness." Though the sixties generation was unusual in that they transformed that feeling, publicly anyway, into a badge of uniqueness and integrity.

They were able to take pride in being unable or unwilling to fit in, perhaps because their sheer number enabled them to see themselves as a majority whose values constituted the norm, as is the case with all majorities everywhere. Perhaps because they grew up in a time of great prosperity they were also enabled to "rise above" values of crass commercialism that so many adults must live by.

They were, in any event, a far cry from a current television star who worked her way into the business by modeling. When asked how she got to the top she replied, "I looked at the business world and identified the markets. I knew the key was that they always wanted someone new. I decided to hit one market one year, then cut my hair and hit another, then let it grow and hit television."

The model's ethos is totally at odds with the values of adolescents generally. To place her intrinsic worth as a human being on such accidents of biology as her face and figure, to devote herself to the most superficial worlds possible, modeling and television, to mold herself into any conceivable "marketable" shape, all of this is anathema to many adolescents who, for all their contradictions, generally insist fiercely upon living in a world of good and bad, deep versus shallow.

Adolescents usually gravitate to the "highest," most idealistic, views of the world. In short, they need a world in which moral ambiguity has been banished so moral certainty may reign supreme. A world in which the "integrity" of one's hair length is inviolable, in which the value of one's job is measured by its intrinsic value to humanity, is a world that is clearly defined, straightforward, and therefore highly reassuring. By imposing rigid values of their own, they make the world more "stable." The chaos of corruption, greed, amorality, and ruthlessness is thereby obliterated.

The confusion adolescents felt, and feel, over the kinds of adults they wanted to be was evidenced by the explosion of the rock-and-roll industry, which they themselves set off. The emergence of rock-and-roll superstars, both then and now, is an obvious instance of an adolescent need to worship and identify with a particular kind of positive model.

For here are persons whose place in society is as ambiguous as their own. They are considered "kids" by the adult world, and indeed, they spend their time in ways not generally considered adult. Yet their poise is limitless. They move about within the adult world with far more adulation, fun, and success than almost any adult who comes to mind.

They do not hold down nine-to-five jobs. Yet they are often multimillionaires. The money they earn enables them to live as only fabulously wealthy adults can. In short, rock stars represent a type of unconscious wish fulfillment on the part of their following, that is, to be a child who successfully wins the respect of adults as well as the prerogatives and the self-sufficiency of adulthood. If it is impossible to see oneself successfully turning into a grown-up one day, the victory or the solution that rock stars find to the same problem is very reassuring.

Adolescents are invariably obsessed with questions about their competence and their chances of being admired and loved. They also tend to think in absolute terms, and feel that they must be either absolutely wonderful or (more often) totally inadequate. They often view other people the same way.

By elevating these musicians to the level of gods and emulating the superficial things that make them stand out (hair length, clothes style, etc.), adolescents manage to transform their own feelings about being different and freakish into something unique and positive, something the older generation cannot understand. When a person is not certain of his identity and has threatening suspicions that there may not be much to him in the final analysis, then he usually will look for someone or something outside himself. By identifying with rock stars, adolescents manage to give themselves a sense of self-worth and competence. It is as though, unable to experience the positive part of themselves directly, they have to imagine someone else has it and then get it vicariously. Years later, when they have a firm grasp on who they are and what they are about, the adulation of rock stars dies. Reminders of the way they used to feel and act seem somehow incomprehensible.

Adolescents generally tend to feel a very strong and a very tenuous surge of godlike omniscience (if evidenced by nothing other than their total rejection of the adult world and the smug superiority with which they dismiss its members). Rock groups provide an outlet for those primitive parts of their collective personalities.

Infants associate their own feelings of well-being with the conviction that they are in total control of the world. They also tend to feel, at some stage in their lives, that they and they alone are what the world revolves around.

At some point in their lives, this reassuring illusion becomes shattered. Sooner or later their world, their mothers, apparently have other responsibilities and relationships that do not include them, such as a husband, other children, jobs, and household responsibilities. A child often is devastated at learning that he is the son, and not the "sun." Without being able to articulate it, this fall from grace, so to speak, is their first experience with their own smallness, their own helplessness. On some level they feel that this knowledge has seeped into their consciousness as a jolting reflection of their personal inadequacy.

When a person again enters the threshold of a wholly new stage of life, which is how adolescence presents itself in most minds, these earlier feelings about the world, and the fear of the second "fall from grace" it involves, come again to the surface.

Hence the conviction in some fourteen-year-olds that the first time they will have a crush on a boy or a girl they must inevitably be rejected.

Hence, too, the elevation of rock stars into a fantasy of perfection and acclaim that most adolescents secretly harbor about themselves. One must remember that it was the adolescents themselves who bought almost every single one of those millions of records. They were the ones who made every Beatle fad a national norm. They were the ones who showered them with incredible adulation at every turn, so much adulation in fact that the group gave up touring for fear of being swamped.

The adolescents, in short, created the gods and therefore the outlet they needed.

There are two other qualities closely associated with rock stars that also provide useful insights into the troubled world of adolescents and that shed important light on the emotional difficulties and impulses that can compel young peo-

ple to take their own lives. The pervasive excitement they
engender and the use of drugs that has become associated
with them deserve our special consideration. For they are
related aspects of a very widespread and serious problem.

The pursuit of excitement, of course, is hardly new or
uncommon among adolescents. As people on the threshold
of the new world of adulthood, they often have a reawak-
ened capacity for sheer wonder. Preparing for careers and
families, choosing between dreams and ambitions destined
to last them, in one form or another, for a lifetime, life
often seems to hold out unlimited opportunities and
promise.

They have also just discovered sexuality. That, to say the
least, is cause for excitement. Among healthy adolescents,
the pursuit is nothing odder or more inexplicable than
their teeming sense of aliveness. It can be generated by any
number of things: a newly discovered passion for a particular vocation or finding that this month's "love of my life"
reciprocates such feelings.

A person, not just an adolescent, needs to be able to become deeply and intimately involved in love and work in
order to grow and find fulfillment. To feel truly alive requires intimacy, with either a person or an ideal that makes
ordinary work seem to be play. It also involves a capacity
to make commitments.

Among many adolescents today, however, the pursuit of
excitement involves few or none of these things. Rather it is
an act of desperation, something they feel in order to escape
their true feelings of emptiness, isolation, and deadness.

As we saw with Fred, the excitement was painful. After
it has been generated, it has to be extinguished, and this may
mean suicide. Analysts routinely see adolescent patients capable of turning this kind of excitement on and off at will.
Anyone who has seen an adolescent in the grip of "false
heartiness" knows how grating and insincere it appears.
There is hardly an adolescent in America who has not spent

time with a peer who has not suffered from this malady in some form, however innocuous. Much like the person who leaps up in the midst of a quiet evening and frantically insists everyone immediately put on his coat (no matter what the weather or distance to destination) and plunge into any number of deadening desperate hours of bar hopping and "partying."

Parents and teachers may themselves know of such youngsters. They are the ones who are never able to form strong attachments, who never find anything that interests them, and above all, who never seem calm or relaxed. "I never feel comfortable unless there's something to worry about" is their quasi-joking anthem. Feeling calm, these youngsters say, makes them feel uncomfortable and strange.

They have a pressing need to generate some kind of intense feeling to stave off more frightening feelings of emptiness. This pursuit of excitement can be hollow and destructive.

Jack had the usual identity problems adolescents face. He did not know who or what he was. He did not know, as he put it, "the purpose of my existence." He was in a perpetual state of metaphysical anguish, which he and his peers often experienced as "an existential crisis."

In spite of his considerable good looks, popularity, and intellectual endowments, Jack was moody, unhappy, and frequently depressed to the point of contemplating suicide. Like many of his peers, Jack contended the world was too difficult to adapt to. His environment was "inordinately complex."

Despite his great successes with girls, Jack routinely withdrew into marijuana stupors and LSD experiences.

When asked about it, he said he found it intolerable to be alone. But true intimacy also terrified him. It stirred up feelings of panic and terror, that somehow he would explode or suffocate if forced to endure what the majority of us have an inexhaustible yearning to have.

He dealt with his dilemma in a disturbing but quite illustrative way. On the one hand, he always somehow found himself making love to his many girl friends when there was somebody somewhere else in the apartment or summer home where he happened to be. No one ever burst in on him, fortunately, but he found the danger exciting. What he did not fully understand was that the tension effectively shifted his attention away from his partner and the intimacy of what he was enacting and onto the peculiar situation itself. During the lovemaking, he incessantly immersed himself in fantasies that he was making love to somebody totally different, somebody he had met under impersonal circumstances, such as a girl he had passed in the student union or on the street just hours before.

His less intimate social moments were also fraught with a desperate and empty pursuit of excitement.

On one level, he did everything possible to avoid being alone, or so it seemed. He was quite gregarious and convivial. He gave many parties, attended social and political functions by the score, found time to take innumerable car trips and nature hikes.

He combined many of these activities, for they obviously were not pleasurably exciting in and of themselves, with a bountiful supply of marijuana.

One of the most amusing and revealing games he invented was candle racing. He would invite his friends over for the evening. Rather than enjoy their company straightforwardly or use moderate amounts of alcohol and drugs to loosen everybody up, he insisted everybody "get wasted."

Assured that the entire group was together but safely ensconced in a marijuana fog, he would then assign each one a candle, which they would light and sit in a circle to watch them all burn down. The one whose candle burned down the fastest won. Admittedly, the image of these young men and women seated around their candles becoming as tense and excited as any gambler at the track is comical.

The pervasive sense of deadness and boredom that lay beneath it, though, can be easily gleaned by identifying with them in a stupor watching a candle burn for forty-five minutes or more.

Indeed, Jack might well strike some, in fact, he did strike many of his peers, as a charming, carefree blade. They were all mystified when they heard that he had been discovered late one night, his wrists slashed, in his shower, nearly dead by the time the ambulance arrived.

In trying to make sense of it all, his friends could only come up with his habit of occasionally slipping into a fog, being "spaced out," as they described it.

Indeed, whenever life became too much for him, whenever the terrible deadness began to infiltrate the seams and fissures of his false excitement, he fell into emotional numbness as a last resort.

For inevitably Jack's friends dropped off one by one in the course of a year. Some became intimately involved with a lover. Others became engrossed in science or art. Others simply did not need, and ultimately could not take, the abolishment of their privacy, the rejection of their need to enjoy themselves alone, which Jack in effect demanded. The girls he chose for sexual partners by and large wanted a closer, more ongoing, more intimate relationship, which he was incapable of providing. Others he discarded himself after the initial sexual novelty, the illusory excitement, wore away.

To Jack it seemed that he could not stand being alone. It would be more accurate to say that he desperately needed to maintain a special kind of total isolation, one in which his inner agitation could be channeled outward through purely sexual and drug-induced excitement. Interpersonally, no one ever got through to him or forced him to experience his inner core.

His suicide attempt took place after he had walked around in a self-imposed "anesthesia" for weeks.

Mary, though she talked of suicide, tried to cope with deadness in another fashion. She used drugs to make the deadness feel like a state of "suspended animation," to turn deadness into a sense of eternal peace and calm. Aside from trying to achieve an occasional mild artificial euphoria, she also used drugs to obliterate herself from the world around her, to deaden her despair and her listlessness.

A true sense of aliveness, we must remember, urges someone on to new experiences. It prompts him eagerly to take on something novel. If a person cannot do this to any significant degree, he or she stagnates. The job, the family, the free time, one's personality itself are all sources of enervation. Everything and everyone is experienced as alive.

Mary routinely toyed with committing suicide, but she did not think of it as shutting out forever overwhelming terrors. Instead she saw it as a natural extension of the deadness that was within her. By ending her life, she imagined she would be reaching a state we call Nirvana. Not cosmic joy, but the sense of serenity in which time stands still and her emotions, the aliveness which self-consciousness brings, would dwindle out.

Like other women who express these feelings, Mary was quiet and withdrawn on the surface but timorous and anguished underneath. The whole idea of seeking something novel, even something comparatively trivial like trying an exotic dish at an ethnic restaurant, frightened and repulsed her. She did not want to be disturbed from her state of "perfect apathy."

Most disturbing of all, Mary did not have the traditional adolescent complaints about cruel, insensitive, unsympathetic parents. She performed adequately in school, had a reasonable number of friends, and felt that her parents were perfectly nice people who cared for her and had done everything they could.

She did admit, however, to one favorite fantasy. She talked about it incessantly to her friends, who to her puzzlement

did not seem to share her enthusiasm. She also spent her
time daydreaming in class, drawing pictures of it in her
notebooks. It was, in short, a part of her which was desperately trying to express itself.

In her fantasy she was in a large medieval banquet hall.
In one corner of the huge room a small orchestra was
playing.

During the performance, Mary was soothed beyond measure by the music while her body seemed overwhelmingly
inert and lifeless. As she listened to the slow and especially
melodic second movement, she noticed, in a detached way,
that she was hungry. The hunger she visualized as a large
peacefully black space within her. Like a sleepwalker, she
would then drift over to the banquet table and fill her
plate with an enormous amount of food. She sat back down
and slowly, calmly fed herself. However, the food, no matter how much she ate, never seemed to fill her up and leave
her with a sense of drowsy gratification. Rather, she ate as
much as she wanted and more, but it did not disturb her
original "soothing emptiness."

What was a deep part of her trying to express? Simply
that the life force, active, aggressive actions that enhance
and perpetuate our lives, and that so threatened hers, could
be experienced safely. Almost everybody, for example, when
undergoing a period of sustained difficulties recoils from the
prospect of a dinner party, a business trip, or an invitation
to break into a new social circle. Situations that would be
pleasantly stimulating when a person feels good about himself become just one more source of painful and noisy ag-
gravation.

Mary felt this sort of thing on a drastic, ongoing basis. She
is only one of many adolescents who suffer from it. Her
fantasy, which she bolstered by drugs to the point where she
nearly failed out of school, fulfilled her underlying need, that
is, to have experiences involving some level of excitement

and still not totally disrupting the deadness that she needed to protect herself against the painful state of aliveness.

Who among us does not know some adolescents who rely upon a steady intake of marijuana or alcohol to "liven up" day after empty and meaningless day of their school life? Their insistence that it makes them feel gay and alive sounds hollow, and it is. What they need most is not nagging and harassment, a version of aggravating, unpleasant noise that drives them ever deeper into an insulated world. They need to be understood and helped.

Unfortunately for Mary, her peers eventually fell out of touch with her. They enjoyed getting out and doing things, and by and by they stopped issuing invitations she consistently refused.

Before the end of her junior year, Mary developed an even deeper problem that all of us suffer from, though obviously to a much milder degree. That is, she became sunk in the morass of her completely private world.

As Joseph Conrad observed, all of us are individual human beings with a private consciousness. No one thinks our thoughts but us. In that sense, all of us live and dream and die alone. Most of us, thankfully, are able to escape what James Baldwin called "the prison of our egocentricity" from time to time. We can lose ourself in work, in family, in love for someone else.

Mary, like a growing group of disturbed adolescents, could not.

Cut off from her friends and family, if only through her own ferocious passivity and withdrawn manner, she had no person who could establish human warmth and contact that would tie her to the larger circle of human life. She went through the motions of attending class, eating, and returning to her vacant room alone. When she was spoken to, she would either mumble something unintelligible or fail to respond altogether. If the person pressed her, she would look up abruptly as though recovering from an episode of amnesia. The person would then have to repeat what he had said two or three times before she responded with a non sequitur of one sort or another.

She got the reputation of being flaky, and since she used drugs, they considered her "a head," the term for heavy users. This description, though benign and accepting in its own way, obviously did not get to, or address, the root of her sufferings.

She replaced her old primary fantasy with another. In this one she pictured herself walking and drifting through an infinitely cold, barren, empty, gray asteroid in a completely empty, pallid universe. She also saw herself take on the shape of her surroundings. Instead of a bright co-ed cheerfully dressed, she pictured herself as a long, graceful, gray water lily floating through her dead universe.

She, of course, invented and created this image herself. Analysts operate on the assumption that people invent these fantasies because they want to express something about themselves in an indirect way that will permit them to get in touch with some hidden part of themselves. Direct revelation without the disguise a fantasy provides might create overwhelming anxiety.

If Mary's fantasy sounds strange and incomprehensible, we need only recall that it resembles almost precisely the kinds of surrealistic landscapes the world-renowned surrealist painter Yves Tanguy composed. The fact that she saw herself as living in an inanimate, lifeless universe all her own was another way of expressing the painful degree to which suicidal adolescents feel they simply do not belong to and cannot find a useful and loving place within the world the rest of us inhabit. Most of us feel alienated from time to time. Mary's sense of alienation was overwhelming enough to feel "cosmic."

She was so painfully uncomfortable with herself that in her dreams she no longer had a human figure, but that of a lovely flower. One evening her friends burst in on her to find her smashing to pieces the beautiful vases and sculptures she had accumulated. When asked to explain what was bothering her and what set off the destructive spree, she shrugged, unable to answer. Shortly thereafter her parents were notified, and Mary was taken out of school and spent the following year working at a department store, living at home, and receiving psychiatric counseling. She ultimately returned to college and finished quite respectably.

In a sense, Mary was one of the fortunate few. She illustrates James Baldwin's contention that people who are absolutely unable to love, respect, or trust another human being live in complete isolation in which they will ultimately commit any crime rather than just endure it. Mary smashed up possessions. She could just as easily have turned those destructive forces on her own life.

A no less seriously troubled group of adolescents are those who build shells around themselves. Unlike crustaceans, these adolescents use their emotional shells to provide a kind of protection against the feelings *within them* as well as protecting them from the world, which they perceive as overwhelmingly threatening.

These human shells, however, are all too often enormously fragile and burdensome. The souls that lay beneath are terribly vulnerable.

Often this group develops what mental health professionals call the "false self." British psychoanalyst Donald Winnicott has pointed out that in most cases the shell represents this false self. It is designed to disguise, protect, and shelter the true self underneath. Optimally, a human being ought to be able to make his inner opinions, needs, and feelings known and respected, making the outer man conform to the inner man. Few of us are well adjusted or lucky enough to live in a milieu that makes that an absolute reality. Those who are fundamentally healthy, though, are, on the whole, able to do so.

When the gap grows greater and greater and the shell becomes more and more artificial, stress and alienation become intolerable.

This is especially true, and especially damaging to adolescents whose sense of self, both true and false, is in such a tremendous sense of flux.

Obviously, the false self represents a way of relating to the environment that has been forcefully imposed by the outside world. Typically, for an adolescent, it involves bending and molds the way one carries on one's life in conformity to someone else's demands. The true self, the real person, is felt to have no right to exist and therefore (in the mind of the teenager), it must be suppressed if not obliterated.

When an adolescent, or anyone for that matter, lives in a world that refuses to recognize and bend to his needs, one's irreducible individuality, one's humanity, is effectively destroyed.

The resulting conformity to what one despises and fears in almost equal measure is, to put it mildly, insincere. Usually it is mechanical and lifeless. Over a period of years, the falseness can be unbearable. What is worse, if it starts early enough in life, people can consciously forget or lose total touch with what they really feel and think. They lose touch with who they really are and go through adolescence experiencing life as filtered through the false self, as something ungratifying, bland, and unreal. Finally a person comes to fear his own feelings whenever they manage to break through. He has come to the conclusion that he has no right to be who he is, that, in fact, expressing that right can be fatal. One feels one must be manipulated by others at every turn. Like the most totalitarian nations, the adolescent's inner "ruling body" considers the true self a dangerous threat that must be cowed or eliminated.

Sometimes such adolescents can seem to be the very soul of compliance (a subject I shall be expanding upon in the next chapter). Other times they become people who are obsessed with visions of robot worlds and cajole their friends with stories of outer space in which, like Mary, they too escape into a universe other than earth in order to be able finally to live in peace.

One of the most striking and saddening instances of such troubled adolescents, however, is the social climbers, the BMOCs, the Big Men on Campus.

These are the persons, such as Carl, who are always seen with a huge, hearty, but insincere smile on their faces. By the time he was a sophomore, Carl had moved into a fraternity house and managed to get himself elected president. Carl was always affable, always quick with a deferential, ingratiating quip, always happy to lend a serious, seemingly concerned, but shallow ear to a troubled fraternity brother.

No one ever saw Carl in a depressed mood or without a convivial, wholesome, interested expression on his face. His father wanted him to follow in his footsteps, and Carl dutifully studied the insurance industry during his college training.

While in school Carl studied hard and at the expense of the usual round of antics associated with college life. Impeccably dressed, always to be seen at the appropriate religious services and youth group activities, Carl "got ahead." He eventually became chief organizer of an annual charity benefit dinner, the vice-president of his class, even the operator of a small student laundry service that provided him with ready spending money (which he invariably banked).

Toward the middle of his senior year, however, perhaps because on some level he could no longer keep the knowledge that his childhood was ending and his false self would by necessity be riveted over him for the rest of his life, Carl began to lose his usual stability.

He told no one, but he began to be deeply disturbed and dissatisfied with his life. He felt that although he knew more people than anyone else on campus, no one really liked him and he was not close to a soul. Nor did he "feel like himself" when he was in company. The laundry concession began to bore him and soon the responsibility, along with his insurance courses, turned into an overwhelmingly tedious chore. Going through the motions became more and more trying, as though he were somehow on Jupiter, where every action required ten times the amount of energy it would on earth.

Then one morning he woke up and could not get out of bed. His entire life appeared before him as one titanic, hollow lie. Afraid to rebel, unable any longer to force himself to conform, he literally could not move. He simply could not go through with the rest of his life. Not knowing how to resolve his conflict, not having anywhere to turn, he finally snapped when some of his fraternity brothers banged on his door asking about him.

He opened his window and leapt out, falling two stories onto bushes and concrete. Sadly, while Carl was in the hospital his father called (a student informed Carl's parents despite his strict orders forbidding that) and asked what had made him do such a thing. Thoroughly cowed by the sound of his father's voice, Carl told him he had been girl watching and lost his balance. Before being discharged, Carl gave himself a pathetic pep talk and "came to his senses." Although he did not end his life—indeed, he became one of the most successful salesmen his insurance company had ever seen—his children today feel he is distant and uninterested in their lives. Gradually, he is on the road to becoming an alcoholic.

What of adolescents who do not fall at either extreme? What about those adolescents who are mixtures of rebellion and compliance? Often these are children who have no physical deficiency. Rather, they have serious conflicts about being successful. They may feel guilty about being more successful than their parents, who have supplied them with their role model for competition. They may be afraid of letting out all the anger they feel toward the world. They have the fundamental talents but they thoroughly hide them from themselves by feeling inferior to their peers and parents.

Parents and teachers often find this group especially bewildering. No amount of reassurance seems to make them feel good about themselves. At the same time, their low self-esteem can be heartbreaking and maddening to witness, because it all seems so unnecessary.

Members of this group often go on to form families and pursue careers. They experience life as difficult and depressing. They may never get over their discomfort with people. They may settle for a vocation that holds no interest for them because they feel too inhibited to pursue what they really want.

No matter how much an adolescent is obsessed with questions about his independence and the rebellion he undertakes to achieve it, he still has his parents playing a crucial and ongoing role in his thoughts. Often a parent, because he does not understand the reason for various kinds of behavior, finds the adolescent incomprehensible. In the subsequent chapter, we shall be focusing on the most common ways in which the clash of adolescent reasoning and adult reasoning results in trauma for both generations.

CHAPTER 6

What Do We Want?

ONE OF THE MOST COMMON STAGES an adolescent passes through is one of rebellion. It is also the one stage that parents and teachers usually find the most exasperating. An adolescent's revolt often seems all-encompassing. Everything about his family, his school, his country suddenly appears unreasonably demanding, unjustifiable, and worthless.

Most adults are probably aware that the rebellion is really a tool adolescents use to say, "Now that I am supposed to be an independent person I must forcefully break out of my childhood mold." In a sense, perhaps the need to rebel is a type of backhanded compliment, for it implies that the adolescent has been supplied with a tangible environment from which he now must separate.

Actually the question of how, or if, an adolescent rebels is a very complex one. It is part of a much larger question, one that goes to the root of the fundamental issue an adolescent struggles with: Who am I? The struggle for an independent identity must be understood in that context, if not by the adolescent himself then certainly by the adults most intimately involved in his life.

More often than not this aspect of the struggle is one of the most explosive, whether or not the explosion occurs openly. This is because adolescents are generally in a period of their lives when they are dealing with tremendously volatile and threatening feelings. They do not have a solid, relatively fixed identity, or to put it another way, they do not have a list of "standard operating procedures" with which to smoothly handle the conflicts they feel. This makes an adult's ability to understand the underlying emotional principles of an adolescent's needs and actions that much more crucial.

In this chapter we shall be focusing on the two most common ways in which adolescents try to deal with this explosive problem, the forging of an independent identity, either through rebellion against the values, expectations, and demands of his family, his school, and his neighborhood or instead through compliance with them all.

For an adult both styles can be equally disturbing though in somewhat different ways.

The overtly rebellious adolescent often inspires exasperation, confusion, and grief in those who are on the receiving end of his revolt. The blossoming of a relatively cheerful and obedient child into an outrageously dressed, enormously touchy, notoriously smug and opinionated, mercurial devotee of crude, wall-rattling popular music can be very trying, depending on one's innate conservation and tolerance level.

On the other hand, those adolescents who fall at the polar opposite, the compliant, can evoke equally unsettling feelings. We have come, by and large, to expect adolescence to usher in a phase of flamboyance, irrationality, and revolt. There can be something very disquieting, therefore, about an adolescent who seems to get along extraordinarily well with his parents. Who continues to do well in school. Who totally adopts the adults' values. Who does not become a member of a "far-out" group and who expresses nothing more than the calm expectation that he will follow in his father's vocational footsteps. What is really going on underneath all that calm exterior? an observant parent might wonder. Is it a rigid mask for feelings that have been violently repressed, and that must someday explode like a time bomb?

Before focusing on the differences between the compliant and the rebellious, it is worth pointing out how they are alike, the similarities in how they look at the world, the similarities of their needs and conflicts, and the common underlying emotional principles at work.

It is no coincidence that adolescents have from time immemorial turned into people very much like their parents. There is no reason to believe it will be any different with the current generation or those that will inevitably follow.

Both those who rebel and those who comply carry the seeds of their parents' values and attitudes within them throughout this transitional phase of life.

All of us have been deeply shaped by the upbringing we received from the man and woman who conceived and raised us. Most of us could count, without exhausting the available fingers on one hand, the number of other people who have had or will have as profound an impact upon us.

This is one major reason why almost all adolescents tend to band together. When children do not know who they are, or more precisely, when their primary picture of themselves is "So-and-so's son" then being off among themselves helps bolster a comfortable and indispensable illusion, that is, that they can be "independent" of their mothers and fathers successfully.

Both groups also tend to look at their parents in a special way. They do not picture them as people more or less like themselves, who have their own flaws and strengths, their own uncertainties, nor as people who were once teenagers themselves and went through much the same emotional upheavals they are undergoing today. Rather, adolescents invariably picture their parents as symbols of authority; a symbol with a personality that is as fixed and unchanging as the North Star. They have very important emotional reasons for maintaining this image, the revision of which is often one of the most painful and important subjects a person addresses in psychoanalysis.

This special parental image, as one may recall from our earlier discussion, is the one adolescents have had since childhood. They needed it then, and to some degree need it today as well, in order to feel they were in a safe and stable environment that protected and cared for them at a time when they could not do so. Most children also learn how to feel good about themselves by first feeling proud of their parents and then trying to emulate them.

This image is of great use to an adolescent, although he obviously does not experience it in this straightforward, practical way. The image reassures that part of the adolescent that is still dependent and childlike, that he is still protected and looked after. It permits him to fix in his mind, and therefore scrutinize, what his roots and his background consist of.

Since learning to be independent and autonomous often involves rebelling against one's own feelings of dependency and childishness, the nearest and most important authority figures make a safe and convenient target.

The plain truth is that regardless of whether adolescents are rebellious or compliant, they are very much, each and every one of them, like their parents. No matter how vociferously they may reject their parents and their standards on some superficial level (e.g., he's dull and opinionated, she's too concerned with clothes and recipes) if one probes a little deeper the common bond of the family stamp is instantly recognizable. This is one reason why after an adolescent has achieved some kind of independent identity, being like his parents is no longer an odious threat. He reconciles himself with the "ogres" and conducts his life in much the same fashion.

What is even more important to our understanding of

adolescents, however, is this: However exalted and idealized an image they have of their parents, adolescents tend to have a self-image that directly reflects the ones their parents have of themselves.

Analysts have been aware of this for years. The evidence is overwhelming. It is supplied by the unsuspecting adolescent patients themselves. Henry may see his father as the most overbearing, self-righteous rock of strength and certainty he has ever had the displeasure of growing up under. Henry may have very low self-esteem and complain bitterly about his inability to match up to his Superman father. In nearly the same breath, however, the adolescent will talk about his father's insomnia or his chronic inability to lose the forty extra pounds he has carried around with him since his teens or his wounds and outrage over the ambivalence his co-workers apparently feel toward him. What is more, our hypothetical and all too typical Henry will be absolutely incapable, at this stage of life, to connect his own low self-esteem with his father's. How can he? Henry needs the image of his father as an authority figure to rebel against too desperately to let his unconscious knowledge reach awareness.

Henry will persist in his temporarily indispensable illusion even if he himself is overweight, suffers from sleeplessness, and has difficulty relating in a gratifying way to other people.

An adolescent's loyalties are typically divided between parents and peers. Often an adolescent himself does not know in precise terms what he wants. Or what his rebellion, or lack of it, will accomplish.

It is no wonder, therefore, that parents and teachers so often throw up their hands, feeling it is impossible to understand what is on an adolescent's mind and what his demands really are. This is one reason why a trivial observation, a stray and meaningless facial grimace, or even a polite request to cut a phone call short can set a fifteen-year-old off. Unable to draw up a list of demands as might a revolutionary cadre, adolescents commonly channel their agitation and confusion into the minutiae of daily life, giving it all emotionally charged, symbolic importance.

If a person wants to move up from the job he presently occupies to general manager of a division, he probably would not go about it by walking into the district director's office, telling him how incompetent he is, how poorly he dresses, and how shallow and repugnant his values are. If this happened, the district director might smile wanly and suggest that his employee seek work elsewhere.

Yet this is approximately the position an adolescent often believes and fears he is in. By this I mean that an adolescent is faced with having to restructure totally his relationship with his parents, go from dependent child to responsible equal. In doing so he is often afraid that he will destroy his relationship with his parents altogether, including the positive and reassuring aspects of it, and thereby leave himself without their emotional support. If we keep in mind that throughout his previous life his parents punished him for "inappropriate" or overly rebellious outbursts, his present irrational fears should not be incomprehensible.

Then too, the very name we give to the process, rebellion, is telling. Those who rebel against a governmental regime must by definition commit themselves to its "violent overthrow." They are labeled traitors and are executed when caught. Of course, restructuring a relationship with one's parents is quite different from destroying it. As an adolescent becomes more comfortable with his capacity for self-reliance he usually comes to recognize that his parents did not intend to block his way after all. In any event, feelings of violent rage do not, in virtually every case, translate into acts of violence against an adult. We are discussing irrational feelings of people who are being launched into the unknown and who have had very little experience with the urges and the forces within and around them.

Still, are there not some adolescents who are so comfortable with themselves, with their families, and with their friends that they can accomplish the huge emotional task of creating an independent identity without either exploding in rebellion or smothering it all?

The answer is yes, but these adolescents present few emotional problems. In order to comprehend why an adolescent does or does not rebel and how to distinguish the normal from the troubled, let us examine a few of the most typical patterns of behavior.

Harold, like many of the adolescents we shall be discussing in this chapter, was the product of an upper-middle-class suburban environment.

His parents were the proverbial influential, prominent pillars of their community. They were comfortably settled. Their dress, their manners, their tastes, and above all their values were what most of us would label the American norm. (Again it should be noted that I have selected this particular socioeconomic group for our discussion because so much of their life-style is familiar to us all. The same problems crop up among adolescents, in about the same proportions, in all other social and economic strata of our country.)

Harold had evolved a way of presenting himself as well as a set of attitudes very much like those of his peers. He let his hair grow long, sported a wispy beard, and confined his wardrobe to ragged, secondhand clothes. He also was violently opposed to the Protestant work ethic and the competitive, materialistic definitions of success.

In fact, Harold was referred to me because he had failed his freshman year of college despite very good high school aptitude scores. Although psychotherapy had been his parents' idea, Harold, on his own, was very eager to establish a relationship with me.

He was desperately seeking relief from intense emotional agitation. What struck me first about Harold was how insin cerely he had assumed the demeanor of what we have come to think of as the typical "hippie" adolescent. Despite the slovenliness of his costume, upon closer examination it appeared remarkably clean and pressed. He slipped into adolescent argot occasionally, but it seemed forced and unnatural, as though it were his father painfully attempting to "relate to the young."

But what seemed disturbing and puzzling was the high regard Harold had for both his mother and father. In his view they judiciously gratified most of his material desires. He did not believe he had been spoiled at all.

Harold's father was a very successful industrialist, and his son took pride in his father's accomplishments. His mother, who could trace her ancestry back to colonial days, was a talented and fairly well-known artist. Harold took pride in her achievements as well.

What is more, Harold believed that in spite of his mother's preoccupation with her work, she was a devoted parent who bestowed more than adequate amounts of time and love and evenhanded care to all her children.

Why then was he so tormented? Simply because he had a strong need to rebel against his environment in order to feel that he was going to be an independent, autonomous person. His self-esteem depended upon being able to accentuate difference, to be able to feel the difference between his life and that of his parents.

Rebellion made Harold feel enormously guilty. Most people know the guilt of lashing out unjustly at someone they love very deeply. How much more magnified must it have been for Harold who, in his own mind, was cutting himself off from and "spitting on" everything the two people who meant the most to him stood for? Infants feel a tremendous sense of gratitude to their parents for sheltering, feeding, and caring for them. A good deal of that gratitude carries over into adolescence as well as into middle age and beyond.

Most people also tend to change their opinions of those they "reject." They revise the former image of a person, perhaps a positive one, in order to support their current hostile view of him. On some level Harold was afraid that by rejecting his parents he would also make his parents worthless. If that seems a bit hard to understand, one need only think of how drastically our opinion of someone and his work changes when we have lost all respect for him. He may be the same person and hold the same job as when we thought highly of him, but after the change, in our eyes, he really is valueless.

From a parent's point of view, Harold's dual needs, to maintain a loving relationship with his parents and to be autonomous, were not contradictory. Rather they were complementary. Every healthy parent wants to see his children as self-reliant adults who ultimately appreciate and enjoy the people who raised them, on an equal adult basis.

To Harold, however, as to many adolescents, such needs feel contradictory. Adolescents, let us keep in mind, tend to think in either-or terms. One cannot have it both ways, the situation seems to say, being both the loving, admiring child and the self-reliant person who acts independent of what his parents' reactions might be.

On an irrational level, Harold did not know what way to turn. Going backward, remaining a child, was intolerable. Going forward, branching out from his parents, seemed too destructive. So, emotionally, Harold was furiously stepping on both the gas pedal and the brake.

Of course it did not present itself to him in this simple, straightforward way. Instead it came in a very recognizable, intellectual form we have seen in other adolescents I have discussed. Harold agonized over not knowing the purpose of his life. He did not know where he belonged. He could not force himself to pursue a particular career (which was, for him, equivalent to gaining an adult identity). He was so afraid of coming up to his father's level of achievement that he did not believe he had any talent. He was certain vocational success of any kind was beyond him.

His life, in short, had become a monstrous self-created dilemma. His depression had reached suicidal proportions. Not wanting to upset and "disappoint" his parents, Harold had become a recluse at college but never shared his distress with them. Had he not flunked out of school, thereby giving the world a clear and unmistakable sign of his torment, he would have continued to gnaw away at himself.

Of course the solid home life Harold had enjoyed throughout his childhood served him well when in therapy. Within a year he was remarkably improved and able to return to school. By flunking out he preserved his identity and perhaps his life. The overriding lesson to learn here is that in order to be independent, this adolescent, like many others, had to rebel, and it did not matter what he was rebelling against. Even those with "all the advantages" often must undergo a stage of "differentiation" from their parents. To put it simply, there comes a time when the very fact that one's father is a model of masculinity and success is experienced as an obstacle. As sages have pointed out, most people feel the need to reject (or "demolish," as they put it) their teacher in order to strike out on their own.

Through treatment Harold was able to realize precisely what his conflict was, and from there to learn that it could be resolved happily. In this case, he learned that his parents expected, and therefore were not terribly threatened by, his need to be independent, to rebel. He learned to change the way he looked at them, coming ultimately to share his parents' view.

More and more analysts are receiving adolescent patients who are severely tormented by parental goals which most of us, at first glance, would label beyond reproach. That is, the insistence that their children be happy, and they do whatever they can to make things right for them.

Sally was such a girl. She had been an active, gregarious

child who became extraordinarily shy, introverted, and unhappy when she reached fourteen. Her parents' concern for her was warm and genuine. Both mother and father were perpetual, compulsive optimists who always made it an article of faith to look on the bright side. Sally's mother was a cheerful, happy sort, while her father had total confidence that his judgment and his behavior were exemplary.

But Sally had a different view of them. She thought of her mother as a scatterbrained and impractical person who somehow had been endowed with a "magic touch" that made everything she did despite her disorganized approach turn out perfectly. Sally had the feeling her mother "skipped through life" innocent and carefree, never knowing pain and suffering.

This made her own torment that much more onerous. It seemed incomprehensible and unjustifiable that she could be miserable in such a home. Rather than making her feel cheerful, Sally found her parents' temperament and outlook suffocating. She recoiled from them both and felt isolated enough to daydream about suicide. The one reservation that held her in check, typically enough, was that she thought her suicide would wound her parents enormously. Sally did not want to hurt anyone. She wanted to be nice.

Sally's parents were both giving and indulgent and made very few demands. They asked her to accept reasonable responsibilities, which she did without much protest. She knew that her parents would take great pleasure and pride in whatever academic achievements she earned. But they did not push her.

They were instead fanatically concerned with her happiness. It was this they seemed to live for and it was this that had become a major conflict in Sally's life. The wish for their daughter's happiness came to be presented as a demand. Sally rebelled against that parental ultimatum, or at least wanted to, as she would have against any tyrannical demand. Her favorite movie, in fact, was one that contained a scene between an arguing husband and wife.

"Just what is it you want?" the exasperated husband shouts.

"For you to stop trying to *make* me happy!"

Happiness, we must remember, is really a by-product of a number of factors. When people achieve a meaningful place for themselves, when they feel that who they are and what they do is meaningful, they feel content and happy. No one, after all, can make you feel anything. Every person, by definition, responds to the people around him, his social life, and the job he does to the degree to which these activities fulfill his expectations and needs. The Talmud states that the rich man is he who is happy with what he has. In America, unfortunately, the right to "the pursuit of happiness" has been as grossly misunderstood as the "right to bear arms."

Sally's lack of happiness, then, was on one level a way of rebelling against her parents' world. It was also an expression of genuine anguish.

Sally was not primarily in the position of someone driven to be unhappy in order to lead her own life. Rather, she was someone who had to refuse to obey a command as to how she was required to feel.

The truth was that Sally's parents were not consciously aware of the insistent nature of their concern and the ways in which it proved counterproductive and even destructive.

In such cases there are no villains and no heroes, just people trying to do their best.

Sally vividly remembered an incident that took place eight years ago (the intensity of the memory alone lets us know its symbolic importance for her). She had been playing with some toy wooden logs her parents had given her. Having halfway constructed a cabin, she stopped to puzzle out exactly what she wanted to do with the next log. She was not in the least confused or lost. She was simply trying to find a novel and unique combination. Immediately her mother stepped over and placed the next log into its "logical" place. She did so assuming that she was being a considerate, involved, caring, helpful parent. She was unaware as she walked off to complete some household chore that she had left her daughter feeling quietly desperate. The message her mother seemed to be conveying was, You do not know how to do anything on your own. Without me you are completely lost.

This incident might have been consigned to oblivion had it not been part of an ongoing total pattern. Sally's father had an equivalent attitude. Sally, an only child, was expected to take over the family-run business. So, although her father told both her and himself that she was free to pursue any career she wanted, all the same he subtly began to manipulate her in that direction. Because Sally was a fourteen-year-old, he could do little more than talk to her at length about his work, take her frequently to his plant, encourage her to be familiar with the staff, and persuade her to take business courses, to join clubs that would expose her to like-minded business-oriented men, to men who would make fine husbands and fine commercial contacts later in life.

Because her parents told her their only concern was for her happiness and what was best for her, Sally, by the time she was fourteen, no longer had any confidence in her own capacity for self-reliance or independence. She had grave, fundamental doubts about her ability to make a decision, hold any opinion, or complete a task successfully on her own. Whenever she had a strong opinion, she could not feel comfortable with it until someone agreed with her. If her parents happened to disagree, she felt both wrong and helplessly outraged.

Sally's dilemma is quite similar to that of Ruth, a fifteen-year-old who had been raised in much the same kind of atmosphere. Her parents were unconscious victims of the cultural values in which they were reared. They were trying to be good parents by following "enlightened" child-rearing guidelines. The fear that their job as parents meant raising a human being who, unlike any others who have come before them or since, would lead a happy, conflict-free life, drove them to counterproductive lengths. Their own desire to do well, their own fear of failure, transformed happiness and doing what was best for their child into a demand they placed upon both themselves and their daughter.

It is hoped that as Americans become more comfortable with formal child-rearing research and writings they will learn to blend these comfortably with their own natural, instinctive reactions.

As it was, Ruth's mother set herself a minimum requirement that amounted to a self-imposed demand that she be a combination of God and the Madonna. She read child psychology books voraciously. Undergoing psychoanalysis during her child's formative years, Ruth's mother was certain that her treatment would make her a more psychologically adept and self-aware parent.

Like Sally, Ruth reached adolescence having nothing to rebel against, on the surface, that is, save for the expectation that she must be happy. Again, like Sally, Ruth felt that she had never owned her own thoughts.

Her mother, she explained, constantly undermined her efforts to do things independently. She did so in such a benevolent fashion that Ruth herself had doubts about the validity of her own instinctive reactions.

To take an innocent-sounding example, Ruth vividly recalled an excursion she had planned with her friends, on her own, to a local amusement park. It was to be an uncomplicated afternoon with a lunch at a nearby hamburger stand.

Ruth's mother approved of her plans and shared her daughter's enthusiasm. Without knowing quite how it happened, Ruth found herself outmanaged and delegated to the sidelines. Her mother insisted upon preparing a large, sumptuous meal for the group. She told her daughter to tell her friends that she would also drive them to the park, make the arrangements for a private table in the recreation area, escort them through the park to make sure they had no trouble with malicious teenage boys or insolent ushers, and finally drive them all home safe and sound.

In her mind, Ruth's mother was a concerned, involved, supportive parent who had gladly, without being asked, sacrificed her own day to ensure her daughter's happiness.

To Ruth, however, whose afternoon it was after all, her mother's efforts had a destructive and depressing effect. A simple afternoon had become a production. The opportunity to enjoy her friends and the freedom from parental supervision was lost. Her own initiative had been dismissed. She mutely went through with the affair, withdrawn, miserable, and resenting every minute. It had gone from something she wanted to do to something she was made to do, no different, in essence, from a Sunday afternoon when she was five years old and her parents ordered her to get dressed because the family was going out to eat.

Ruth, over the years, developed intense shyness, a reaction to an instinctive feeling that she could do nothing correctly. She developed absolutely no confidence in her ability to execute a project by herself.

She felt, in short, an abiding sense of inadequacy and an inability to be on her own.

At this point the reader may well shake his head and mutter, you can't win! Even active parental involvement is counterproductive. On the surface that appears to be the case. It would be more correct to say that nine times out of ten rebellion is normal, healthy, and predictable. Many adolescents need to rebel, and parents and teachers should be able to anticipate it and, as long as it is not destructive, to tolerate it as well. While an adolescent might be strident in his opposition to something in particular, a parent and teacher would be mistaken in failing to look below the surface for the real purpose of this rebellion. Adults who have confidence in the love and the home life they provide can usually count upon weathering the rebellion.

At the same time, there is a very big difference between being helpful and being unbearably intrusive. It is hardly a matter of negligence or overindulgence to solicit and respect adolescents' views and to let them decide how they want to live their lives. It goes without saying that if one's child announces his intention of buying a motorcycle and flying it off a cliff to prove his theories of weightlessness, one has to intervene and prevent it. On the other hand, by cultivating some selective sense of "benign passivity" one can help to fortify a child's sense of self-worth and independence.

It did not occur to Ruth's mother that her daughter would have been much more gratified by conducting a simple outing on her own. In this case, that is precisely what would have been best for her daughter. Surely an adolescent has much callower views and opinions than her parents. The basic issue is not the parents' intellectual sophistication or personal tastes. It is a sense of respect for the adolescent himself. We must keep in mind that a parent's approval means a great deal to an adolescent. That extends to a parent's acceptance of the child's being entitled to his own mind, to feel that his parents have fundamental confidence in their child's good judgment.

If rebellion is inevitable, then, it would be more comfortable for parents to be willing, within prudent limits, to accept it and convey to their children that they are able comfortably to withstand it. The adolescent may be worried that if he expresses his outrage and his insolence, his parents will never have anything to do with him again, but that is not how most understanding parents feel.

If Ruth's mother had simply asked herself whether her daughter might prefer to manage her excursion all by herself, she would have preserved her daughter's pleasure, her self-esteem, and had the rest of the afternoon free for herself. Whose needs, then, was Ruth's mother truly fulfilling?

The need to be different often compels adolescents to immerse themselves in ideologies and interests that are antithetical to those of their parents. The son of a conservative stockbroker may immerse himself in Marxism, Buddhism, punk rock, and conceptual art. It is not always easy for a parent to realize this can represent a healthy appetite for new experiences, the willingness to enter into worlds the adolescent was never exposed to as a child.

The adolescent may also find them stimulating in their own way and they may all prove helpful, as his disenchantment slowly sets in, in helping him learn to decide for himself what he believes in and the kind of person he wants to become.

The fact that these are areas that may irritate and mystify the father can also be useful for the adolescent's emotional development, if not for the short-range climate of the household. This does not mean a good father should be intolerant just for his child's sake. Rather, the adolescent's ability to experience himself as different from his father frees him to strike out on his own and conform later on by choice.

What about those who are compliant? Often teenagers who live quiet, unobtrusive lives view themselves as strange. They perceive their behavior as different from some elusive norm, for example the mythical, wild-eyed, supremely secure rebel. They cannot find the security and the self-esteem they need. They imagine that if they fit the image of the fed-up and misunderstood adolescent, they would receive it.

Many times the compliant adolescent suffers just as much and is victim to the same anguish as the overtly rebellious teenager, even though it may be hard for family members to perceive it.

Psychiatrists who practice in upper-middle-class suburbs are continually struck by one form of this kind of suffering.

I refer to adolescents who have incorporated their parents' own "rose-colored glasses outlook" and made it their own. (This syndrome is by no means unique to the suburbs.)

It can be characterized as a cheerful, artificial, forced optimism. The people who suffer from it are invariably polite and nice to the point of being saccharine. They seldom say anything derogatory about someone else. When they disagree with a person they always make allowances and become apologists. They equate feelings of anger, resentment, revenge, lust, greed, all the cruder impulses, with something bad and hence something good people do not or should not feel. Their parents moved to the suburbs, in many cases, to escape the uglier, seamier sides of life so often found in an urban environment. Just as their elders fled from this aspect of life, so do their children have enormous difficulty in acknowledging it themselves.

This forced and unrealistic view of the world, which implies an enormous discomfort with it, translates many times into a way of acting and judging oneself that turns out to be even more difficult and destructive.

Sooner or later, many of the adolescents who through the years have gradually emulated and wholly adopted their parents' rosy outlook, their hypocrisy, and their fears, find their façade unbearable, without knowing why.

They become uncomfortable with these kinds of adults. They become especially sensitive to artificiality without knowing how to break out of it.

When they get to college many of them are embarrassed to admit that they come from comfortable and highly insulated neighborhoods. Their rebellion may take the form of wanting to plunge themselves into a ghetto, in some reportorial or social-work capacity, to see and experience "real life firsthand."

Psychiatrists who treat these youngsters discover over and over that they feel they have only a "skin-deep" relationship with their mothers and fathers. Parents who construct an emotional straitjacket that does not permit them to frankly face the fact that they are more devoted to their careers or their social groups than to child raising (because such an admission would mean they are "not nice people") inadvertently do their children a great disservice.

A child, like anyone else, knows on some level whether he is truly wanted and cared for or not. It is very threatening indeed to feel that one is unwanted. To live in a household where the truth is perpetually denied, where a child is perpetually told that he is the apple of his parents' eye when something deep down inside tells him he is not, may in the long run be even more destructive.

As an adolescent whose father deserted him when he was two years old observed, "I had it easier than some kids because as far as my father was concerned *I always knew where I stood.*"

Those who have the capacity to rebel openly against such parents (and it is worth stressing again that we are talking about a subgroup that cuts across class lines) are in fact rejecting something very concrete and specific.

That is, they are trying to permit the emotional truth about their lives and those of their mothers and fathers to come out into the open. Being different may take the form of acting depressed, grim, and insecure. Unlike their parents, who have learned successfully to cope by putting up a false front, these adolescents stop trying to do so. They feel their parents' underlying insecurity within themselves and have made it part of their own identity. They lack the motivation and the tools to disguise it.

On the other hand, there are those children who do not have the ability to rebel openly. Jim was such a child. He was brought up in a very affluent West Coast suburb, a place where a great deal of emphasis was placed upon academic achievement and professional accomplishment. Jim's father had been born into an immigrant, Depression-era household. He had known economic deprivation as a youth and had overcome it through enormous amounts of hard work and business acumen. By the time Jim was three his father had been so successful that the only tangible incentive Jim had to someday surpass his father's achievements was emotionally motivated. The incentive born of poverty was gone.

His father left the house before Jim got up and usually came home from the office an hour or so after Jim fell asleep at night. When he was very young Jim was vaguely haunted by the feeling (for this is how children reason) that he was responsible for his father's absence, that there was something bad and inadequate about him that caused his father to avoid him.

When his father was home, invariably executing some leftover work in his study, Jim did not spend much time with him. Even so, his father prided himself on how bright and intellectually precocious his son was. He also prided himself on how much he had done for his son, how many material advantages he supplied him, and how much he cared for him.

Jim's mother also shared her husband's views. She told Jim over and over as he was growing up how much his absentee father was involved in his life. Although she too had a business career to pursue and put that task at the forefront of her own sense of self-definition, she told Jim, like a propaganda campaign that never varied, that he was the most beloved boy on the face of the earth. In practice, though, she was not fundamentally more involved with Jim than was her husband.

Everyone who was most important to Jim was talking in rhapsodies about love and attention, but in reality no one showed any. In the final analysis, their own careers invariably came first, but not because they needed the money, although all their efforts went into accumulating as many material comforts as possible while telling Jim and all their friends that it was really only spiritual values that mattered.

The reason for this was that on an unconscious level, their own self-esteem and their own priorities revolved around work in the marketplace.

Given their own by no means unique or isolated gifts for self-deception, it is little wonder that Jim wound up a very lonely, unhappy, unloved child. He was raised under the delusion that he was getting the best there was, and there was no room in the universe of his home for the frank admission that this was not so. On those few early occasions when Jim somehow lashed out incoherently in a plea for love, his parents were astounded, one might say blinded. What do you mean we don't love you? they told Jim. How can you feel so unhappy when we have sacrificed everything for your happiness? With an amused smile and a shrug of their patient understanding shoulders, they blinded themselves to his anguish and ignored his plea.

Jim began to experience difficulties in his sophomore year of high school. He rapidly became an introspective A student who seemed to pick up quickly on the intellectual and emotional conditions surrounding him.

The lack of love conveyed on a primitive level when he was an infant now came back to haunt him. He found himself unwilling and unable to form any relationships with his peers, either boys or girls.

He funneled all his energies into mastering physics texts and scientific principles and maintaining a rigid schedule. Those around him failed to become concerned when they noticed that he violently objected to anyone's touching him. The mere possibility of accidentally brushing against someone else, the most fleeting human contact, sent him into a fit of terror and rage.

By the spring of that year he had become an intellectual machine spitting out lucid answers in class and answering questions or greetings from classmates with esoteric, incomprehensible puns. His parents, when they noticed his refusal to be touched at all, dismissed it as simply an adolescent phase he was going through. His classmates and teachers thought of him as being temporarily eccentric, as so many students are from time to time.

Finally, though, his inner conflicts converged and overwhelmed him. His budding sexuality was pushing him toward intimate human relationships, which he had learned would be denied him and which he therefore must not seek. Yet the sheer force of his inner emptiness and despair made his need for love all that much more acute. At first he was unable to reach out for help, but by now he was unwilling even to make the attempt. So one night he sneaked into his parents' basement. He loaded the gun his father concealed in the cedar closet and put a bullet through his head.

To those who knew him he appeared to be relating adequately to the world. Had he been just a bit more severely disturbed, had he been a bit more eccentric or suffered a breakdown, his problem would have been recognized. His parents, though unable to admit their own responsibility, would finally have had to come to terms with it, if only by sending him to receive psychiatric help.

How many Jims are there currently in America? No one knows precisely, but we do know that they exist in sufficient numbers to prompt us to reexamine carefully our attitudes and our possible complacency.

Jim's case is not meant to imply that there are not parents who are paragons of self-confidence and self-esteem. They do, indeed, exist and tend to pass those qualities along to their children. They are, regretfully, the exceptions. This may sound discouraging. However, it should not come as much of a surprise to anyone who has had enough experience dealing with people to have reached the private conclusion that the vast majority of adults have moderate amounts of uncertainties and insecurities.

Some analysts, unfortunately, tend to react to the volume of disturbed youngsters and adults they see in treatment by feeling a private sense of outrage against the parents who

raised them. That assuredly is overly simple and at any rate
is not the point of the discussions here.

Suicidal youngsters, however, often come from troubled
households. It is important to stress that the factors that
produce overwhelming emotional difficulties are complex,
interrelated, and, above all, a matter of degree.

The vast majority of adults have various mixtures of
strengths and weaknesses as parents. They are not all good
or entirely bad. I know for instance a young man who, at
the age of three, interpreted the birth of a younger brother
as a personal rejection by his parents. His parents were well-
meaning, loving people who had no idea that their oldest
son would feel responsible when the youngest fell very ill
at the age of two months. The child concluded that only
by being sick and weak and helpless could he capture the
attention and emotional energy his mother had to devote
to the ailing sibling.

As an adolescent, the older boy attempted to take his life
over a problem he was having in school. It makes no sense
to blame anyone. Our energies are better devoted to trying
to unearth the sources of emotional difficulties, to recognize
symptoms, and to help these adolescents through greater
understanding.

All children develop an "image," a way of behaving in
the family that serves to tell them who they are and what
they "have to do" to be loved. The roles vary, of course.
Some children assume the role of "the scholar," while others
may be "the perfect child." As adolescents, however, children become more self-conscious and begin to question the
image they have cultivated. Often they become resentful
and bitter in it.

Compliant adolescents, the ones with the ever nice and
obedient images, often suffer acutely. They feel trapped,
afraid to let their feelings of hostility or rebellion or unhappiness show because they imagine they will be severely

punished or deprived of the parental love they so badly need.

Compliant adolescents may never have learned that it is permitted to express anger. They may have no experience in acting in any other manner. In some cases they may fear that if they stop being compliant their families may fall apart. In some cases this fear is quite realistic.

Becky was a compliant adolescent who became unbearably depressed at the age of twenty. She could not point to any specific cause for her problems, which made her turmoil all the greater. She felt constantly harassed. She felt that life was making crushing demands on her.

When she became obsessed with taking her life she came to me for treatment. In some ways Becky epitomized the seemingly puzzling rash of suicides afflicting middle-American homes. She was very attractive and intelligent. She was engaged to a promising young man quite devoted to her. She was going to pursue a career in law, for which her teachers predicted great success.

Her father was a very prominent lawyer. Becky was an only child born into a close-knit, large, extended family. On the surface she seemed to have everything. Her parents did not expect her to pursue the traditional female role of housewife. They had always assumed that she was going to be a lawyer.

It was only when she was well along in her law courses that Becky felt serious conflicts about her chosen career. She woke up one day and asked herself what she really wanted to do with her life, and she could not come up with an answer.

Once in therapy she began to talk about feeling that her parents resented her being born and that "in retaliation" they put her to work as a servant, used her as a confidante and adviser, a sort of parent to her mother and father.

Her mother in fact was a markedly dependent and insecure soul who had a drinking problem. She had encountered serious and nearly fatal complications in giving birth to Becky, which unfortunately she told her daughter about over and over during Becky's childhood.

To the outside world Becky's charm and innate intellectual ability left the impression that she was happy and in control of her own life. Just below the surface, though, Becky had the pervasive feeling that she was responsible for her mother's emotional problems. Becky's role, as she saw it, was to protect her mother and serve as her one source of solace and comfort. This was not entirely fantasy. For without Becky the mother would at some point have had to be institutionalized to stop drinking and to pull herself together emotionally into some semblance of self-reliance.

Since this was the way Becky grew up, since this is how she was raised to feel she had to relate to people, she naturally anticipated serving her law clients in the same fashion. As the perfect daughter, which is how both she and her parents saw her, she imagined that all her future clients would be equally doting and equally unable to function without her.

As an adolescent, exposed for the first time to the world, she became aware of alternative roles. She no longer thought it important, or even healthy, to be the perfect daughter. She realized that she had not found filling her mother's needs personally satisfying. She did not relish the prospect of continuing that pattern throughout the rest of her adult life.

She also began to feel, quite rightly so, that her parenting was not in her mother's best interests, since in practice it did not help her to become healthier and more independent. In fact, it really kept her from facing up to the magnitude of her problem and therefore kept her from seeking professional assistance. Not surprisingly, Becky also grew to resent her father for acquiescing and encouraging her to assume unreasonable and unhealthy responsibilities.

Finally, she realized that she had grown up feeling that

her responsibilities, one might say ironclad obligations, to others had neither a beginning nor an end. She felt she had never been given a choice in the matter, and she began to be furious with herself for being too fearful and guilt-ridden to openly resign her traditional role.

The closer she came to getting her law degree, the more she doubted whether she had any choice in this matter either. Since it had been assumed almost from birth that she would be a lawyer, her high grades and enthusiasm for law itself could not assuage her abiding suspicion that this too had been forced upon her as the good, compliant, perfect daughter who had spent her entire life fulfilling her parents' wishes at the expense of her own.

Her treatment, as it turned out, was her first sign of healthy rebellion. That might sound odd at first. However, it was the first major step she had ever taken toward voicing her own concerns and soliciting the counsel of someone outside the family. Her father was a practical, concrete-minded person who opposed psychotherapy as an unnecessary indulgence.

Becky made tremendous progress. She had developed great inner strength and self-reliant qualities growing up. These served her well in achieving her own sense of purpose. Within a year Becky decided for herself that she wanted to be a lawyer. She passed her bar exams, married her fiancé, and, rather than taking her own life or succumbing to her guilt by continuing to serve her mother's destructive needs, she managed to break away and pursue a gratifying career.

Conformity usually means a person has to deny his own needs for the sake of another. For Becky, it meant that at the time she was struggling for her own identity she was fundamentally unable to sort out whether what she did was from choice or from guilt. Her parents, unable to recognize the bind they inadvertently placed her in by making her feel guilty about refusing to care for her mother, were not able to do what was healthiest for all concerned.

Since I have been discussing what we can consider to be representative patterns, it is worth noting that parents are just as capable of being disrupted by an adolescent's demands.

When Ernie returned from college after his freshman year, he had become an evangelist with what we may call a "subsistence living."

He dressed in the most modest fashion. He spent his summer devoted to helping the poor and reading innumerable tomes about poverty, all from secondhand bookstores, in his spare time. He confined himself to a strict, simple, vegetarian diet. He either walked or used public transportation. Above all, he rejected plush surroundings and luxuries of all kinds.

Since his parents lived in an affluent suburb, a philosophical conflict became inevitable. Ernie did not harbor great contempt for his parents, nor did he want to break with them.

On the contrary, he wanted to convert them to his point of view. He wanted them to abandon the life they had built for themselves through long years of hard work and live as he did. His attempt to "reform" them carried a far more pressing emotional meaning for him. Ernie was a depressed youngster who had considered suicide before immersing himself in his new philosophy. By proselytizing and earnestly working to convert his parents and friends, he gained a sense of identity and purpose. It gave him a reason to live and made him feel much more alive.

Beneath his urbane, sophisticated manner and materialistic life-style, his father also had many of Ernie's present convictions about how one should live and how one should be in touch with suffering humanity. In his own youth, in fact, his father had been nearly as idealistic. The more he listened to Ernie, the guiltier he felt about the "absurdity" of his own life-style.

Rather than being fixed in his values and outlook, Ernie's

father began to feel more and more uncomfortable with the life he was leading. He was a child of the Depression, someone who had been forced to be extremely thrifty and who had to do without. His father, Ernie's grandfather, had been a sharecropper.

No matter how much he agreed philosophically with Ernie, he could not bring himself voluntarily to undergo the deprivations forced upon him as a youth. It had not been easy reaching the point where instead of tormenting himself over whether to begrudge himself some inexpensive pleasure he now could afford to spend money freely and enjoy the things it bought. He had spent years taking streetcars and he did not intend to give up his luxury sedan for the bus now.

In a sense, then, the traditional parent-adolescent roles became reversed. Ernie stood over his father and demanded that he conform to a particular set of values, a certain rigid life-style. His father responded by feeling that he had the right to lead his own life the way he chose to! He was not forcing his values on Ernie; why should his son not grant him the same freedom?

Several years later, after watching his friends move on to lucrative careers in advertising, law, medicine, and other professions, Ernie gave up his life-style. For Ernie, as with most all adolescents, the issue of rebellion is not a nihilistic rejection of society and family but an indispensable element in the process of turning oneself into a self-reliant adult.

CHAPTER 7

We Die So We May Live

His fat round face wore a grieved and bewildered look
like a child who had been so sternly treated at home it
did not expect better from the rest of the world.

KATHERINE ANNE PORTER

WE MUST NOW TURN to perhaps the most controversial
section of our discussion, that is, to mothers and fathers who
harbor unconscious, destructive attitudes toward their children, which sometimes drive their offspring to take their lives.
As noted earlier, it is a problem that is generally avoided.
If we are to do the pressing subject of adolescent suicide
unflinching justice, we must address it comprehensively.

Perhaps the most common problem confronting parents
in dealing with troubled adolescents is the refusal to admit
that one's child is having difficulties that go beyond the
boundaries of the "normal teenage problems."

Parents do not have any monopoly on denial. There is
hardly a person on earth who does not find some aspect of
his life so painful that he deals with it by putting it out of
his mind entirely. The small investor who cannot admit that
the stock that contains his life savings is going to continue
to decline, a newlywed who senses her husband is "staying
late at the office" because he is conducting his first extra-
marital affair but cannot bring herself to confront him about
it, the middle-aged son who refuses to see the deterioration
of his elderly father because the imminence of his death is

too painful—all these people use denial to avoid facing the reality of their situations.

Parents of troubled adolescents may say to themselves that their children will outgrow their current difficulties, that they have been raised properly so that nothing could possibly be wrong with them, and that anyhow adolescents must learn to work out their problems as their elders had to. That is all part of growing up.

It is terribly painful to admit that one's child suffers, let alone that he or she may be disturbed.

No one wants to see his child in pain. Furthermore, many people cannot help but feel that the way a child turns out is a direct reflection on the parenting he received. No one likes to be told that he is unattractive or incompetent on the job. How much more magnified are the feelings when they concern one's parenting?

It is still true that the vast majority of people do not equate physical injuries with emotional ones. If a person accidentally closed a door on a child's finger, he would not deny that it took place because it was a direct reflection on him. Nor would he consider his child's injury a figment of the child's imagination, something he would outgrow. For that matter, he would not worry about what other people thought of him as a parent if they found out he had to take his child to the hospital emergency room to repair the injury. The reverse is normally true when it comes to accidental emotional injuries. In some cases, unfortunately, denial results in an emotional injury that never heals properly.

I shall be examining some of the warning signs of serious emotional difficulties among adolescents, signs that a child is potentially suicidal, later on in the book. For now we need to underscore how important it is to take an adolescent's turmoil seriously. It is a common and very serious mistake for parents to feel that an adolescent's problems are not as "real" as an adult's. In some ways, in fact, an adolescent's problems may be more serious simply because he has not yet had the experience in coping with large problems.

An adult, for example, may look at a teenage boy depressed about losing a race for class president and dismiss the magnitude of his suffering because it does not have the same serious consequences as his father's highly mixed employee evaluation submitted last month. The student lost a meaningless election, the reasoning runs, but his father lost a raise needed to support his family and he may lose his job altogether. Unfortunately, that kind of reasoning fails to take into consideration that the son, perhaps suffering from low self-esteem in the first place, has just endured a mass rejection, something akin (in his mind anyhow) to everyone he knows standing up and saying that they think he is unattractive and that they like somebody else much better. Depending on the person, the adolescent may be humiliated and devastated enough by the election results (as we saw in the opening section of the book) to attempt to end his life.

His father, by contrast, would probably be capable of enduring the trauma if the very worst occurred, and after a few months of turmoil seeking a new job, he would be able to put it all behind him.

None of this is to say that one should hover over a child relentlessly wringing one's hands over every disappointment. The principle involved here is to be able to acknowledge how important such matters are to an adolescent. For all his defiance and insistence that no one understands him, an adolescent gains enormous relief from seeing that a parent takes his identity problems seriously (a theme I will be expanding upon in our conclusion). However insensitive one's son may claim his parent is, he is usually very hungry for a parent to treat him and his crisis as worthy of adult respect. It conveys a sense of dignity to the adolescent, a sense that he is on the road to being a legitimate adult with legitimate concerns, rather than an ineffectual and useless person whose pain is not to be taken seriously. It is best to let our children know we take their problems as seriously as we take our own.

One of the rewards for this attitude is that one can build upon it while being in better touch with one's child. One of the inadvertent penalties a person may pay for a lack of this appreciation is a breakdown in communication and resentments that may lead to a very poor relationship when the adolescent reaches adulthood. If the denial and the lack of appreciation are too severe and the adolescent feels increasingly alienated and lost in an overwhelmingly painful world, the result can be suicide.

Analysts, for example, frequently find that a person's early experience in puppy love leaves an indelible impression that may fester in the psyche well into adulthood. Parents tend to dismiss puppy love with an amused shrug when they are not outright indignant about it.

For the adolescent, puppy love is a very serious matter. His whole life may revolve around the relationship. Although he may not put it this way, to him, it symbolizes many things. It usually is his first acquaintance with the powerful adult emotion of love. It may be his way of tentatively experimenting with his own incipient adulthood status, as well as a way of testing out how desirable and lovable he is in his own mind.

The vulnerable adolescent may feel totally devastated and humiliated if the affair is abruptly terminated. A parent who fails to see nothing more than two fourteen-year-olds who are no longer going steady runs the risk of missing the warning signs of serious emotional turmoil that the aftermath can bring to the surface. Responses such as "Grow up," "Pull yourself together," "What's the matter with you, there'll be others!" sometimes amount to little more than sticking one's head in the sand rather than facing the possibility that the adolescent has significant difficulties that prevent him from shrugging it off.

A fifty-seven-year-old industrialist, during the course of his psychoanalysis, returned continually to the unresolved traumatic experience of his first attachment to a girl, which occurred almost forty-five years earlier. He always talked about the first girl he had ever loved with a tremendous amount of feeling.

Looking back, he did not find her particularly attractive. He had never even kissed her. Nevertheless, like Joseph Heller's protagonist in the novel *Something Happened,* he remembered the affair in detail and replayed it in his mind obsessively.

What stood out in his mind above all was the summer vacation after his freshman year in high school. The girl was vacationing at her parents' summer cottage, and sometime during July he told his parents he was going to the resort area to visit a friend. He neglected to tell his parents whom exactly he was visiting, and they thought nothing of the matter inasmuch as the objections they had to his girl friend (based on her coming from a lower social class) did not apply to his male companions.

After he departed, his mother ran across a note from the girl saying how much she was looking forward to seeing him. Although her son was barely thirteen years old, his mother immediately assumed that the two were planning to elope. She worked her husband up into a frenzy, and he phoned his son at the summer cottage to inform him that he was driving down immediately to take him home.

Petrified with shame and fear, the son hung up without a word of protest. Had he been able to sink down into the middle of the earth, he would gladly have done so. How was he supposed to explain his imminent departure to his hosts? "I'm sorry, but my parents consider you socially beneath us and therefore are coming to remove me from this inferior setting"? "I didn't tell my parents exactly whom I was visiting, and since I'm only thirteen and not old enough to be with girls, my parents are taking me home"?

His father whisked him away, but that was not the end of

the matter. Today, in his middle fifties, he was still capable of feeling a nearly uncontrollable rage against his father. The point here is that a child's first romantic experiences also represent an attempt to create a healthy, normal sexual identity. In their own minds his parents felt they were doing what was best for him. In reality they were threatened and outraged that their son would take steps to evolve a life of his own, to begin the slow process that would end in his "deserting" them.

The prospect of a child's growing up and leaving home, in fact, is often the basis for the most explosive, destructive unconscious feelings some parents can harbor toward their offspring. The reasons for this are complex. The intensity of feelings can cover a broad spectrum. It can compel parents to attempt to block a child's romantic efforts. At its most destructive it can result in unconsciously murderous feelings toward one's own child.

Parents who are afflicted with these kinds of feelings are victims of an unhealthy need for a child's dependency and admiration. They do not experience the inevitable growing-up process as a personal achievement. A son's growing autonomy is felt to be a rejection, that he is somehow abandoning them.

Probably all of us, at one time or another, have caught ourselves exclaiming in a moment of exasperation, "I could kill that son of mine!" or "I could cheerfully strangle her!" This does not, I hasten to add, mean that one has serious and pervasive murderous feelings toward one's child. The troubled and destructive parents I am discussing here are those who, for example, may have been seized by jealousy over the attention a child has received from a spouse since birth, as though the love lavished upon him to ensure his survival is at one's own expense.

Children of parents with murderous wishes sometimes respond by killing themselves. Having been raised in such an atmosphere, they usually suffer from low self-esteem and raging self-hatred. When they take their lives, they often do so with their parents very nearby, as though they were simultaneously trying to fulfill their parents' unconscious desires while inflicting as much guilt and grief upon them as possible.

It is important to keep in mind that destructive feelings toward an adolescent can be the outcome of one's own sense of inadequacy rather than of overtly brutal acts.

Some parents with low self-esteem need constant reassurance that they are worthwhile. Unfortunately, since fundamentally they are afflicted with the conviction that they are no good, the reassurance, once given, rarely has any effect.

A father, for example, who does not consider himself lovable may find it impossible to feel secure in his relationship with his son. If he does not hear from him because the son is busy with exams and other activities at a distant school, he may interpret this as a sign of rejection and neglect. When he does receive a call, he is likely to complain that his son is ungrateful, self-centered, and indifferent. He may add that the only way to prove him wrong is for the son to drop everything and come visit now. The message is clear. The father, having no confidence in the relationship or in his own attractiveness, instinctively relies upon guilt to acquire what he does not think he can get in any other way. Unfortunately, by doing so, the father creates his own vicious circle. He wants a command performance and that is exactly what he gets. As his son grows older and more resistant to such manipulation, he naturally finds ways of avoiding his father. He resents and flees from the source of unreasonable guilt. In the meantime the father has the opportunity to complain, with great accuracy, that his son calls him only out of obligation, not love.

Some mothers, whose self-esteem depends upon receiving constant reassurance, unconsciously use their children in order to feel comfortable with themselves. They need to feel important (as we all do) and they try to receive that feeling through their offsprings' accomplishments.

From all outward appearances, these unfortunate, insecure parents often appear indistinguishable from healthy, doting parents. They treat their children as prize ornaments. Everything their child may do, from infancy on up, must be celebrated exhaustively. But at the bottom these parents are desperately trying to celebrate a *positive reflection of themselves*.

The distinction I am drawing here is a very subtle one. It is normal and healthy to take pride in a child's accomplishments. Doing so is a first step toward helping a child learn that doing well for his own sake is perfectly acceptable. It threatens no one in the household. It is one basis upon which a child learns to feel competent and good about himself. Through a parent's healthy pride in his child's accomplishments, the offspring learns that he is loved for who he is, whether or not he achieves great academic and professional success.

Contrast this with the attitudes of the insecure mother I have been discussing; the results of her kind of "pride" can be disastrous. Anyone who has, as a child, come home with a report card one grade short of straight A's only to be hounded by the words "Why not an A in penmanship?" probably went to sleep that night, and many nights thereafter, feeling like a complete failure. Such a mother has inadvertently telegraphed her own feelings of inadequacy and her fear of failure to her children.

One might well ask, But doesn't this kind of mother give her children something to strive for? Perhaps. More likely though, these types of expectations amount to considering perfection a minimum requirement. It is as unrealistic to require perfection of children as it is of parents. The secure and supportive parent places the main emphasis on the achievements the child has demonstrated.

Insecure parents, without realizing it, respond to their children with attitudes based upon their own insecurities rather than on their offsprings' inadequacies. These children sometimes become adolescents who are convinced that nothing they do is good enough. They may not rebel. They are driven, but unable to take pleasure in the accomplishments they do achieve. Needless to say, they tend to experience their parents as taskmasters or sources of guilt rather than of love and understanding.

Such children, unfortunately, often have had traumatic early childhoods. Again, from a distance their mothers seem to be anticipating their offspring's every need even before the child can express it. In reality the child often experiences the overabundance of attention as unbearably suffocating and assaultive.

Being fed when they are already sated, being entertained and jostled when they are weary and want to sleep or simply to enjoy a few moments of solitude can produce feelings of fear and frustration just as intense as those of children who are deprived of even minimum amounts of attention.

A child who somehow senses that his mother cannot tolerate the threat of his independence can easily grow up feeling that he is totally responsible for his mother's mental balance and that only by his remaining dependent can his parent survive. When this kind of message is relayed from virtually the moment of birth, it becomes so ingrained that it is next to impossible to step outside the situation, and realize that being cared for is not synonymous with being needed to live. To be under someone's dominance is equated, in the child's mind, with being loved.

If such children are gifted they often protect themselves from these kinds of parental onslaughts by cultivating their precociousness. As adolescents, they may appear self-assured to the point of smugness. They can be aggressive and successfully enterprising.

However, those traits often are skin deep. They conceal

deep feelings of underlying helplessness and vulnerability. When these children find themselves in situations where their arrogance is not tolerated, as they inevitably will, their true fragility comes to the fore and they cease functioning smoothly.

Analysts see many of this type of potentially suicidal adolescent. They invariably feel themselves to be nothing more than a reflection of their parents. They have neither a sense of being autonomous nor of having the inner wherewithal to evolve that feeling. As a result, they do not feel any purpose to their life.

Still other adolescents who have endured intrusive upbringings become high school students who are obsessively on guard against attack. This, in fact, is a reflection of how they see the world. They are often fanatical about preparing for the next day's schoolwork, not out of a hunger to excel but to overcome an overwhelming fear of being devastated and humiliated by not knowing the answer to questions.

Analysis is most effective when a patient allows the seemingly random flow of thoughts to proceed without deliberation, thereby helping painful buried emotional problems to be expressed. These adolescents, by contrast, often find that process threatening and try instead to prepare everything they are going to say in advance.

Questions by a teacher are invariably interpreted as a challenge or an assault. Young men who have this type of conflict often develop a fascination for the martial arts, such as karate or judo. Being able to defend themselves against all comers with their bare hands, without the assistance of weapons, is crucial to them.

Clinical experience over the past few decades has made us aware that there are familiar patterns that develop in certain troubled households. In a family where the mother is acting in a suffocating and destructive way, the husband is often a passive and ineffectual man who is unable either to recognize the problem or intervene to correct it.

Clinical experience has also shown that a mother often cannot help but convey her feelings about herself to her children, so that they come to see themselves as their mother sees herself. The secure and self-confident mother (or father for that matter) often implants those traits in a son or daughter. On the other hand, a mother who hates herself can have a destructive effect upon her children. Indeed, parents who hate themselves often fall victim to hating their children as well. Often it comes as an unconscious equation that runs something like this: "Nothing connected with me is any good, and since my children are indisputably flesh of my flesh they cannot be any good either."

Such parents may find themselves from time to time hating their children without wanting to, "for no reason." They may not put it to themselves as straightforwardly as I have here. Rather, they are likely to hold lingering, persistent private thoughts that their children are inadequate or damaged and not as good as other people's children.

Often they appear to care diligently for their own children and push them toward achievement. They see themselves as trying to give their sons and daughters self-confidence. The children themselves, though, hearing a steady litany of their shortcomings over the years, learn instead that nothing about the way they look or act is attractive. In short, they come to hate themselves bitterly, and this bitterness (given the opportunities adolescence provides for humiliation, rejection, and shame) may explode into self-destructive acts.

These are the adolescents who do not believe there is any reason why anyone should like them, the ones who suffer the tortures of the damned around members of the opposite sex, the ones who believe they are naturally inferior and inadequate and therefore can look forward to a life consisting primarily of failures.

Self-hatred and a peculiar sense of revolt against an assaultive parent sometimes combine in an adolescent, with the result that the child, most frequently a female, contracts a psychosomatic illness that can end in death. I refer to a condition called anorexia nervosa, in which the sufferer may give up eating, sometimes claiming that she is far too overweight. This particular disturbance, as many readers may know, has been receiving increasing attention from the general public and medical community alike.

Research into this illness actively continues. It is not a well-understood entity. Its symptoms are showing up more and more frequently among adolescents. In its most severe forms, the sufferer loses up to 40 percent of her normal body weight. She ceases menstruating and, unless she receives medical help, may starve herself to death. No matter how thin, how emaciated she becomes, she often maintains, at least to herself, that she is overweight.

An anorectic's refusal to admit what she is really doing in the face of her parents' protests should not be surprising. The first, and often the most difficult, step for an institutionalized adolescent to take is becoming fully conscious that she is in a mental institution. Once she can openly admit that she is there because she is emotionally disturbed, she has, in effect, permitted the healthy part of her psyche to get the upper hand and confront the problem directly. The same admission usually is the first step toward recovery for an anorectic, who frequently has to be institutionalized.

It is my conviction that anorectics are being overwhelmed by the very primitive parts of their mind. On some fundamental level the sufferer typically resents her dependence upon the world, or rather the most basic source of nourishment, food. Since everyone's very first source of nourishment is mother's milk, the food normally stands in the child's mind for the mother. To refuse to eat is to be free of any dependence upon one's mother. The more a mother protests her child's refusal of nourishment, the more upset the mother becomes at the rejection of her meals. For the child, there is a feeling of gloating and revenge at a mother's helplessness and frenzy. This feeling is not so very different, one might add, from that of the young man we met earlier whose ultimate fantasy had him sitting on a sheet of ice, immune from the attempts of others to break through to him and to apprehend him.

Nor is the refusal to menstruate without meaning. It is simultaneously a way to keep from growing up and a way to remain free of sexual feelings, which so often propel us beyond our rational control into unfamiliar situations.

It is important to note that just as some of us get depressed from time to time without being what an analyst would diagnose as clinically depressed, so too can an adolescent girl refuse to eat temporarily and even miss a menstrual cycle without being considered an anorectic. Anyone who is concerned about an adolescent who may suffer from ano- rexia nervosa should consult a mental health professional immediately.

Having discussed self-hatred, we can now turn to another major emotional conflict that can drive adolescents to sui- cide—guilt over one's competitive urges.

As mentioned earlier, everyone's early urge to "replace" the parent of one's own sex in order to have the other one all to oneself ultimately becomes transformed into a desire to be like that parent and then to be "better than" him or her. In the unconscious mind of the adolescent this can present a conflict. For it seems a very ungrateful thing to do, "destroying" the person who has been the model for a sexual identity and who has in fact conceived and raised him. Besting or demolishing one's very first and most important "rival" would also mean (unconsciously) destroying the per- son that one is almost totally dependent upon for love and survival.

Since most of us naturally expect every "wrong" action to bring about an equal and opposite reaction or punish- ment, it would seem that the penalty for destroying someone else, or symbolically doing so by outcompeting them, would be death. Or a feeling of guilt, which, as with Ross Lockridge, urges someone to take his own life.

As a child of seven, Tom could remember feeling that his parents were the most wonderful and glamorous people in the world. As their son, he thought he was the luckiest person on earth.

His parents had been deeply committed left-wing unionists involved in politics during their youth. They had been members of the Communist party and had first met during a cell meeting. After a brief, intense whirlwind romance, they had settled in a grim working-class neighborhood and taken blue-collar jobs in order to help establish strong unions. In short, they presented the sort of idealistic models some adolescents dream about.

Tom was raised during the fifties, a threatening period for anyone with a leftist past, but Tom remembered it all as a highly adventurous time in which he was entrusted with important secrets about his parents that he was never to reveal. By the time Tom entered high school, his father had become a seasoned labor attorney, while his mother rose to a powerful post in a union where she was a dynamic and effective leader. His parents were both highly intellectual and attractive people, and Tom was an unmistakably precocious young man, both mentally and physically, by the time he was fifteen.

There were, however, difficulties. Like many people who find comfort and a life's purpose in an ideology, his parents were much better at empathizing with human beings as an abstract mass than as individuals. They provided a home life for Tom, but they related to him most comfortably on an intellectual level rather than an emotional one. His father had all the oratorical and analytic gifts that make for a first-rate lawyer. His father also had very high expectations of him. He lectured incessantly about the law, about the strategy and the machinations of political campaigns. He also used the "cross-examination" approach to refine Tom's thinking. This had a devastating effect upon Tom. Desperately wanting to please and emulate his father on the one hand, on the other he developed a terror of being unable to come up with the right answer. Living up to his father's ideal for him meant that he always had to be prepared, that his father might try to "catch him in a lapse," to "attack" him at any time.

While Tom was growing up his mother held down a steady job by day and was normally off doing union or political campaign work by night. Hoping to instill self-reliance in her son, she placed the responsibilities for cleaning house and cooking dinner in his hands as soon as he was old enough to carry them out. She became quite irritable if she found the home dusty or the meal unprepared when she returned home at night.

She was from the generation in which men were not expected to participate in the running of a household. Her husband adamantly refused to do so. Tom's mother deeply resented the double demands of worker and housewife that she was expected to shoulder. A good measure of her bitterness and frustration was inevitably vented on her son.

As Tom entered his junior year, his father took on ever more responsibilities in his firm, and soon he too was gone in the evenings, often spending a week to ten days on the road lobbying for reforms in the state capital, arguing cases for clients in other towns, and strengthening the firm's political influence through the banquet circuit.

At this time Tom became consumed by school affairs. He worked like a demon to bring home straight A's. He also became embroiled in a variety of extramural controversies with the administration. Using the techniques he had picked up at home, he organized and led a highly disciplined student protest against the prevailing dress code. Within months it was changed and all students from then on could attend classes in jeans. He went on to organize another protest against the shockingly low number of minority staff members. More were hired.

Like his parents, he too began coming home late at night. His parents, however, while expressing pleasure in his work while on their way to or from a meeting of their own, somehow conveyed their feeling that it was not as serious a victory as those they themselves had fought for. His father especially, feeling that his son was somehow on the road to outdoing his own record, invariably switched the subject from Tom's eager tales to his struggles. When he did talk to Tom about his activities, it was in the "cross-examination" style, which made constructive suggestions come in the form of pointing his "deficits" out to him. The more successful Tom was, the more "seriously" his father examined his tactics, and the more errors he was able to point out. His mother, on the other hand, suffering from the absence of her husband, turned to Tom as the one "adult" ear in the house to tell her own troubles to.

Matters came to a head for Tom that spring. He decided to run for president of the student council. When his father heard of this, he dug out from the attic a box of old campaign buttons that bore his last name, souvenirs of an old union race he had won in his younger years.

Needless to say, Tom's campaign surpassed that of the competition. His address to the school body was, for a high school student, amazingly sophisticated and rousing. Not quite seventeen, Tom had become president of the council and in the process had achieved the most impressive record of activism the institution had ever seen.

He came home that evening to an empty house. An important bill was up for a vote in the state house of representatives. His mother was embroiled in a crucial aldermanic race. Neither parent could be immediately reached, and when Tom managed to inform them of his victory the next day they could barely acknowledge it in the crush of their ongoing job pressures.

Quickly, without being able to chart the changes himself, Tom became more and more withdrawn. He began to avoid his friends and cut short any conversation with a curt remark. At first he went through the motions of doing his homework and then stopped altogether, hardly aware that his grades were slipping. Soon it became a major effort just dragging himself to school every morning. The thought of having achieved his high office left him guilty and uncomfortable, as though it were some dreadfully painful and traumatic event. At first he was able to force himself to attend meetings and chair them, but gradually he forgot about some he had scheduled and would call up another office-holder at the last minute, asking him to run it without him. He spent those hours chain smoking outside the school and staring off into space.

One day he took the afternoon off, bought some razor blades at the corner drugstore, and went home and fatally slashed his wrists. Tom had been caught in the whiplash of his own conflicting emotions. On the one hand it seemed that nothing he did, even achieving a position that both his mother and father looked to, in their own lives, as the ultimate, was enough to win their approval. He had become active, as far as he was concerned, to meet his parents' needs, specifically his father's expectations of him.

On the other hand he had succeeded beyond his own wildest dreams. Neither of his parents had had as great an impact on their environment as he imposed upon his own. On an unconscious level he had outstripped the man he wanted to please most. It was as though he had won the lead part in a play nobody wanted to see. Success, inasmuch as it was rewarded with an empty house and lip-service congratulations, seemed to be cause for punishment. All his dynamism was really only a cover for his enormous vulnerability.

Tom, of course, is an extreme example. His feelings were in some ways a magnification of a quite ordinary experience. For who has not long dreamt of attaining some goal or award that he imagines is going to make him at once loved, admired, and special, only to find that once he does reach it, all he feels is an aching sense of emptiness as though it were all a sham, a fake, a joke all along.

The opposite type is also common among adolescents. That is, adolescents who appear to have all the gifts for success but who are never able to put them to positive use. Many times they indeed have more than enough talent to succeed, but they harbor terribly low feelings about themselves, feelings that to the outsider seem so unnecessary and unjustified by "the facts." Frequently, these adolescents are afraid of doing better than their fathers, often because the elders have somehow conveyed the message that they are superior and have the first and last word about every matter. They subtly let a child know, even if they are not consciously aware of it, that they consider themselves direct competitors with their children and would feel humiliated if their children outdid them.

Madeline, for example, developed a love of literature and writing as a sophomore. Urged by her father to pursue it ("Don't just talk about it; submit your work to judges and see what happens"), she won two creative-writing contests in high school and was included in a national anthology of promising young high school writers. But within the year she grew depressed about her interest and decided to become a nurse instead. Perhaps her father was not entirely responsible for her precipitous drop in self-confidence. However, after Madeline won those contests he began to become terribly concerned about her welfare, a concern that translated into a steady stream of angry questions about how she planned to support herself writing when virtually no one in America is able to. He pointed out that she was not being practical, that there were no jobs for fiction writers ex-

cept in the Soviet Union. At one point, in fact, as the whole
family was sitting around the dinner table, he cautioned his
wife not to discuss his professional affairs in front of his
daughter because he "did not want to be humiliated when
he read it all in a book someday." This comment, interest-
ingly enough, was a backhanded way of granting her a sort
of success that at the moment was beyond her wildest
dreams.

Still other adolescents attempt to cope with feelings of
competition and an inhospitable home environment by trying to create an environment of their own.

Larry was such a person. He was the extraordinarily gifted
son of a very wealthy and famous man. It is worth noting
that an adult's notoriety and success do not, by definition,
spell trouble for ambitious offspring. There are people who
can successfully convey to their children that there is plenty
of room in the world for them to accomplish much more
than they ever did and that in fact they take more pride in
their children's accomplishments than their own. The
French author Alexander Dumas, upon receiving a note
from his son (who had also become a famous writer) on a
recent success, replied that of all his creations his son was
his finest masterpiece.

Larry's father, unfortunately, was one of those outstanding
successes I referred to earlier. Without consciously intending any harm, he took such great pride in his accomplishments (which the whole world appeared to echo) that he saw
himself as a splendid role model, a source of inspiration for
his son.

Since the father felt that any product of his could not
help but be superior, he was not terribly concerned when,
at the age of nineteen, Larry dropped out of school. To outsiders it was a mystifying decision. Larry was an extremely
adept and creative physics student, so gifted, in fact, that he
was permitted to structure his own course of learning. The
faculty was amazed when Larry flunked a physics final; they

even offered to let him retake it and expunge the failing grade from his record. Larry would have none of that. He left the city, moved to a remote rural area, and bought an old farmhouse with money he had received from a trust fund his grandfather had left him.

He invited half a dozen friends, all school dropouts, to join him, and together they started a small candle-manufacturing business. The business soon prospered to the point where his friends invited their girl friends to join them and a small commune was established.

What would make someone like Larry, an industrious and sophisticated physicist, make a complete turnaround and choose a life-style totally insulated and different from what he knew? Obviously there were great emotional conflicts at work (as the subsequent events shall demonstrate). Without realizing it consciously, Larry was attempting to save himself by constructing an alternate world that somehow had to find a place in the larger surrounding one.

In the commune, he was treated as a genius (an important point inasmuch as his father was revered from about the time Larry was born). The people with whom he lived held his business ability in the highest regard. They also turned to him for group therapy to help them work out their personal and interpersonal problems.

He held regular sessions in which everyone there unburdened his deepest fears, thoughts, and vulnerabilities. He was so skillful a counselor that he soon had the reputation of being a charismatic leader as well. When adolescents outside the commune heard about him they too joined. Within a year he headed a fairly large community. He trained others to become group leaders, and it appeared for a while that everyone was content.

As lurid newspaper accounts of far more disturbing cults have made clear, self-contained communities like Larry's seem to carry the seeds of their destruction within themselves. The "secondary" population ultimately proved transient.

At bottom they were not as prepared to withdraw perma-
nently from the greater society as was Larry. Some stayed
during their summer vacation and returned to school in the
fall. Others remained for a year at most. Even his inner core
of disciples periodically returned to their homes for a visit.
Gradually even his "true believers" returned full time to
the larger world.

While it lasted, Larry's farmhouse became, in essence, a
"psychiatric clinic," an out-patient institution in which the
former physics student was the esteemed and revered director. As the population dwindled drastically, Larry became
agitated and testy. He confided to one of his group leaders,
somewhat bitterly, that people had the right to do what
they pleased but at the same time he was disappointed at
"what little backbone" they had.

More significantly he went on to confide that as the son
of a famous man he had always been destined for great
things. As a boy he was always reminded by adults that he
could look forward to following in his father's footsteps. He
was always known as "the famous man's son," never as a
person in his own right. No matter what he did he was always compared to his father and his immense accomplishments. He was never permitted to feel that he could measure
up to him, let alone surpass his achievements. In short,
there was no getting away from him.

Larry did not make the obvious connection, which was that
the only way he could live with himself was to create a separate world in which he occupied a place as important as his
father did in the real one. Nor could he take, unfortunately, a rational view of the panic he felt when he saw his
miniature society crumble. It was as though his failure to be
an important and independent person as a child in his father's house was being replayed on a permanent basis in
the initial years of his adult life.

In short, the desertions drove home the unbearable realization that no matter where he went or what he did, he

could never establish an independent identity and a professional career remotely on a par with his father's. Two years after he established the commune, with only two members left, Larry hung himself. Strange and tragic as his destiny may sound, it is by no means unusual among charismatic adult sect leaders. The mass murders of which these leaders are capable may well have roots in severe emotional conflicts. Their homicidal acts are mystifying and horrible to the public. It is probably fair to say that they turn their hatred and murderous impulses toward "deserters" and themselves.

How can a concerned adult recognize the most typical warning signs of a suicide attempt? What informal and practical steps can an adult take to assist a troubled youth? It is these questions that we are now in a position to address in our concluding section.

PART THREE

How Can We Be Helped?

Thus I draw from the absurd three consequences, which are
my revolt, my freedom and my passion. . . . It is bad to stop,
hard to be satisfied with a single way of seeing, to go
without contradiction. . . . The preceding merely defines
a way of thinking. The point is to live.

ALBERT CAMUS

CHAPTER 8

How Can We Be Understood?

> You are so young, so before all-beginning, I want to beg
> you, as much as I can, to be patient to all that is un-
> solved in your heart and try to love the questions them-
> selves like locked rooms and like books that are written
> in a very foreign tongue. Do not now seek the answers
> which cannot be given you because you would not be
> able to live them. And the point is to live everything.
> Live the questions now. Perhaps you will then gradually
> without knowing it live along some distant day into the
> answer.
>
> RAINER MARIA RILKE

IN TRYING TO UNDERSTAND ADOLESCENT SUICIDE and prevent
it before it happens, we should keep in mind that the majority of those who attempt suicide do not truly want to die.

Like a convoluted and intricate cat's cradle, the suicide
attempt represents a challenge for the adult who can, hope-
fully, be able to help an adolescent rework a destructive
way of life.

In the past, much has been made of the distinction between
those who are and those who are not serious about ending
their lives. It is true that in most every instance someone
who is fanatically committed to ending his life will find a
sure means to do so. There are indeed those who fall into
this category and who were discovered by what seemed to
be accidental circumstances before it was too late. In those
cases, they are institutionalized for extensive periods of time.
They suffer from what mental health professionals call se-

vere deficits, which means simply that their personalities are so fragile and that they have entered adolescence with such gaps in their emotional resiliency that they may be clinically unable to function on their own.

There are others who do not have these absolute deficits, who may be potentially suicidal, but who are capable of going on to very gratifying adult lives.

This does not mean, however, that we should simply dismiss those who are not serious. It might comfort us to draw a line separating the truly suicidal from the acting suicidal into two neat groups, but it really cannot be done. People do almost everything for a variety of motives, and attempting to take one's life usually carries with it a mixture of meanings. A small part of the determined person's mind may secretly wish that someone would intervene or that the circumstances driving him to a fatal act would arbitrarily change for the better. Just as important, those who are basically involved in life have enough of a truly self-destructive drive to do something that could potentially kill them. Anyone who tries to kill himself puts himself in a position where he may likely succeed. Even if he does not, in the sense that the means he chooses do not appear overwhelmingly lethal, he has developed a way of relating to the people and the events in his life that is dangerous. While other people deal with their problems in a constructive and assertive way in order to find the peace of mind resolution brings, the suicidal adolescent tries to resolve his problems by killing himself.

For that reason alone we should never minimize and belittle the seriousness of the act itself. By so doing we not only ignore the facts but we run the risk that an adolescent may someday be driven to actually kill himself to prove how seriously troubled he really was.

Are there any warning signs that give us clues that a young life is in danger? As noted earlier, people are not mathematical equations or computers. We cannot point to any absolute signs, but we can outline broad, relatively detailed categories of behavioral changes and traumatic events that can serve to sharpen our concern.

The first dictum to destroy is the prevailing myth that anyone who talks about taking his life will not do so. Talking about suicide is a way of asking, crying out, for help. If that cry is ignored, under the illusion that as long as someone just talks about it he is sufficiently venting steam, a self-destructive act may well follow. There are reasons why people who are considering suicide do not talk about wanting to. The reason other people do talk about it is often that they are desperately hoping for someone mature and concerned to become involved in their lives before the despairing part within them proves overwhelming.

Observations have also shown that many adolescents who have attempted to kill themselves experienced a wild and drastic mood swing shortly before the act was committed. Puzzling as it sounds, the swing was often from dismal despair to exhilaration. In the past they had been apathetic, morose, withdrawn, and depressed. Suddenly, they became active, interested, and hopeful about the future. Relatives and friends were lulled into a false sense of optimism perhaps because they were not truly in touch with what was going on within the adolescent and therefore were just happy enough to see whatever it was that made the child miserable disappear.

In a psychiatric ward, for example, the personnel become especially cautious when a chronically depressed patient suddenly and arbitrarily appears to snap out of his unhappiness. The reason for this is that true emotional equilibrium is constructed gradually, piece by piece, like a building. Violent mood swings are just opposite sides of the same coin, the same deeply troubled human being's psyche.

As we have seen, a variety of different types of adolescents give in to the urge to die in a variety of different situations. All the attempts, however, have one factor in common.

Something in his environment has changed (his family, his school, his relationships to peers), which makes the way in which he normally adjusted to life impossible. We might list the most common traumatic changes as follows:

Separation　A friend may move away and no one else may realize how much the adolescent depended upon such an intimate relationship for solace, advice, and empathy. No one, in fact, may even be aware that the friendship existed, let alone that it provided an indispensable link to coping in the larger world. The loss of a friend may be just as desolating, emotionally, as the loss of a lover and evoke the same sense of being all alone in the world, uncared for and unnoticed.

Separation crisis can also be provoked, as we have seen, by the loss of a steady boy friend or girl friend. One's whole world and much of one's self-esteem can revolve around the feeling of being loved and needed, the sense that one can be attractive to those outside the family circle, who in an adolescent's mind may love him because "they have to." Studies have found that the most traumatic emotional loss people of all ages endure is the loss of a loved one.

The loss or separation of a close family member through death or divorce can also have a devastating effect upon an adolescent.

The loss of a familiar environment also represents a separation that is often a highly disturbing event. It can come in the form of a graduation from elementary or high school. In these cases an adolescent may not have been totally happy in the old milieu, but he at least knew how to fit into it adequately. Leaving one of these institutions sometimes involves involuntarily severing a relationship with a deeply trusted and beloved teacher or counselor. For adolescents who have a history of being vulnerable and depressed and who have a great deal of difficulty either adapting to unfamiliar situations or making new friends, the move can be traumatic. A child can feel just as alone and helpless as if his family had all perished suddenly, even though the beloved teacher may live in the neighborhood and the institution the child now attends is only a mile or two away from the old one.

Disillusionment As I have discussed earlier, adolescents have a tremendous need to embrace ideals and worship authority figures that give them a solid system of values to cling to. The more passionately they believe in a particular system or person, the more tenuous their inner security may well be. When Larry's self-created environment broke down, the low self-image he had seeped through and overwhelmed him. When an adolescent cult follower discovers that his beliefs, and by extension his adherence to them, are false, the structure on which he based his existence has also collapsed. The same can be said of a hero who has proven to be all too mortal or venal.

Any adult who has seen everything he believed in turn to ashes knows how devastating this can be. Newspapers routinely carry stories describing the suicides of wealthy middle-aged people who abruptly endured the evaporation of their fortunes or the bankruptcy of the companies they built from scratch in their youth.

Parents and teachers, therefore, who may well recognize the fatuousness or the insipidity of an adolescent's devotion to a particular cause or leader, make a great mistake when they ridicule the infatuation itself. The adolescent is better served by the adult's focusing on the child's need to idolize and trying to understand the wellsprings, which is to say the emotional uncertainty, that drive him. No adult enjoys hearing his political opinions, his clothes style, or the manner in which he lives belittled, even if it comes from an adolescent "wet behind the ears." An adolescent, however, is often desperately unsure of his judgment no matter how smug he appears. The belittlement by authority figures is often interpreted as a crushing rejection of the person who holds the beliefs and not the ideology itself.

When the idealized belief or leader is reduced to dust, adolescents also experience it as the loss of something in themselves, something about themselves that was once valuable, perhaps the only thing about themselves they thought was worthwhile. In the past perhaps they were able to keep themselves emotionally together by identifying with the strength and the virtue of the religion or movement.

Adult insensitivity There is no one thing in and of itself that causes someone to end his life. A particular incident serves more like a straw that breaks the camel's back. With all the conflicts and pressures adolescents normally face in trying to create an independent adult identity, the camel's back metaphor is unusually apt.

Parents or teachers who make light of the distress an adolescent feels about a rejection, the loss of a friend, a poor grade report, or the sudden fascination with an ideology may accomplish nothing more than making him feel totally cut off from the world. Such a response may serve to accentuate the terribly painful feelings of being odd or different. It may well dam up the turmoil, permitting the pressure to build and build within the child until he explodes in a destructive act.

The hostility with which a parent or teacher treats an infatuation with a fad, even something as trivial as a new kind of popular music, may leave some vulnerable adolescents feeling foolish and "unworthy" of adult consideration. This does not mean that one must adore every trend an adolescent endorses simply because he has developed a momentary taste for it. Rather, a respect for the adolescent's right to his own tastes and the bare-minimum credit one might offer a stranger with interests at variance with one's own permit the child to feel more secure about himself. He may, in fact, rush home and offer to play a particularly jarring piece of insipid music. To ignore the opportunity to become closer to the adolescent, by permitting him to share something very precious, simply because one prefers Vivaldi or Telemann, can be terribly hurtful to a child.

As I have stressed, however, it is unrealistic to see oneself as absolutely empathic or totally insensitive. Like the emotional turmoil an adolescent may be vulnerable to, these traits are all a matter of degree. An adult who attempts to be "perfect" in his relationship to an adolescent is being as unfair to himself as is a teenager who expects that he must be the perfect child.

It is impossible to see directly into the heart and the mind of another human being. It is difficult enough being able to see unflinchingly into one's own psyche. It is reasonable, however, to aim for a fairly comprehensive overall understanding of what an adolescent's ideals and aspirations are.

If a parent knows nothing about these things, this in itself may be an ominous sign. To some degree adolescents may be taciturn and secretive. Adolescents often feel conflicted over "being grown up" and "living at home like a kid." They may feel embarrassed about their dependence and therefore keep their ambitions to themselves as a way of compensating, as a means of feeling that they are independent souls.

Nevertheless, an adolescent who shares so little of himself that no one in the family has any idea of what is going on in his mind may actually be acting that way because he is threatened by his parents. That is, he may be afraid of their disapproval or belittlement. All the more so if a major part of his own mind is unsure about the efficacy of his plans. Without realizing it, an adolescent may be unconsciously afraid that inner revelations will bring a parental reaction that confirms his own darkest fears about himself. Without realizing it, he may even go so far as to put his parents into the position of censor by interpreting a chance remark as vicious condemnation.

The danger in this is obvious. For if an adolescent feels that the people who are closest to him are officers of an inquisition, he may cut himself off from the two most important sources of support and love he has. Similarly, parents and teachers who demonstrate no perceptible interest in a child's enthusiasms may also have a destructive effect.

It sometimes happens that an adolescent cannot help but feel his parents are unacceptable as confidants. He may feel that his mother, no matter how concerned, "makes him feel like a baby" if she asks him how he is and what he plans to do with himself. On the other hand, almost all of us have some painful memory of our father sitting us down to ask "what your plans are." In retrospect we can probably now see that his intentions were good and responsible. At the time it could well have seemed that we were being put on the spot, as though the Judgment Day gavel was waiting to fall if our answer failed to "measure up" or our uncertainty seemed too vast.

Here the overriding principle is that an adolescent should have some adult outlet, some authority figure with whom he can comfortably share his concerns. A parent may not be the sole source of comfort and solace, but as long as the adolescent is receiving that kind of empathy from an equivalent figure (such as an aunt or a guidance counselor), the adolescent is assured some type of healthy outlet and by extension a way of staying in touch with the world around him. If a parent is concerned about an adolescent's close-mouthed behavior it is a sign of empathy, not defeat, to ask if he would like to talk to some other adult on an ongoing basis. Such a suggestion in fact may well make it easier for an adolescent to seek counsel. With an overly withdrawn adolescent one must be empathic and make certain that the most immediate emotional need is addressed.

There are other questions an adult can profitably ask in trying to gauge an adolescent's emotional well-being. Does the teenager look forward to new social and intellectual experiences? Does he have enough confidence in himself and enough of an appetite for life to meet it enthusiastically? Again, we are dealing not with absolutes but with overall patterns. If an adolescent cannot bring himself to go out on a date, to attend a school social event of any kind, to place himself in new situations, he may have seriously emotional insecurities.

Adolescence, after all, is a time in which one is supposed to be testing out the ability to conquer new challenges. It is by racking up some modest series of successes that one gains the self-confidence to tackle the ever greater ones of adulthood.

Those who have a strong urge to live are people who have generally clear notions of what they want from life. They are able to define relatively realistic goals. They are able to establish expectations and needs that can reasonably be fulfilled.

Adolescents often have the wildest possible expectations of life and of each other. They base these feelings not so much on experience as upon their ideals and their fantasies (being short of experience and long on ideals). Adolescents often have considerable difficulty reconciling how they want to live and what their goals ought to be with the very solid limitations of the real world. It is not easy to come to the realization that no one human being can make anybody totally and perpetually content. As adults we have all had to learn this the hard way, and very few people can completely give up the wish that it were possible.

To a degree, every person has to go through the various kinds of reality training life imposes on its own. An adult should be aware of what an adolescent's expectations from life are and be able, with empathy, to act as a supportive buffer through the difficult moments. At the very least, an adult should have some sense of when an adolescent is placing a dangerous amount of expectation of future happiness on a situation that cannot possibly provide it.

In any event, adolescents desperately need adult assistance in surviving these gauntlets. They gain, for example, a tremendous amount of reassurance, security, and relief from parents who acknowledge the importance and the intensity of their concern. This means treating seriously questions like Who am I? and What is the purpose of my life? An adolescent is far less likely to feel overwhelmingly peculiar or lost or alienated when a parent is able to listen in a nonjudgmental way. It is also helpful to keep in mind that alongside an adolescent's confusion is a great desire to find his way in the world.

In this vein we must also keep sight of the fact that the vast majority of adolescent suicide attempts are meant to convey a very powerful and primitive emotion to someone very close to them. In many cases the suicide attempt represents massive anger, hatred, or a thirst for revenge.

Just as one of the young girls I discussed earlier hesitated to take her life because she "did not want to hurt her parents," there are others who try to take their lives for exactly that reason. "They'll be sorry they treated me this way!" and "You drove me to my death and now you'll have to live with it!" are some of the rationales. Author Philip Roth provided a grotesque fictional example of this kind of motive in *Portnoy's Complaint*. In it he discussed an adolescent boy torn between wanting to please and wanting to revolt against a domineering, guilt-producing mother. Roth's intent was as bitter as it was satiric, and he had the boy hang himself with a note attached to his shirt telling his mother to return a neighbor's phone call.

Still others may attempt suicide as a way of demonstrating how troubled they feel, as a means of calling a "time-out" to a daily family life that is not responding to or cannot cope with the child's turmoil. Again, it is tragically counterproductive to dismiss or belittle these attempts because they are histrionic. The more sophisticated adults are in their approach to adolescents, the more likely they will be able to detect suicidal intent.

Adolescents often make suicidal attempts that, on some level, are intentionally designed to fail. They are ways of saying, "I do not know how to cope adequately with my life. I am overwhelmed but I do not really want to kill myself in order to receive help."

Marion, for example, was a seventeen-year-old girl who took an overdose of pills. Before doing so she made arrangements for her girl friend to call her that afternoon. She took the phone off the hook, in her mind perhaps to prevent anyone from interrupting her, as she was about to slip into total grogginess. When her friend called at the appointed time and received a busy signal for an hour and a half, she grew alarmed. Her friend was very close to Marion and knew that over the past three weeks she had been unbearably depressed. She rushed to Marion's home, found her in a comatose state, and arranged to have her taken to the hospital, thereby saving her life.

Marion sent out a very subtle and indirect signal, which only someone very close to her, someone very concerned about her survival, would be able to interpret correctly. In a larger sense this is what many adolescent suicide attempts are desperately trying to convey.

Georgia presented a similar challenge to her parents. For extended periods of time she was chronically depressed. When in the thrall of such moods she would answer questions with "Who cares?" or "What does it matter?" and "Why bother?" Much as her parents cared for her, a seemingly unending diet of despairing, indifferent remarks, listless behavior, moping, and a fiercely long face nearly drained them of whatever energy they had. Georgia did not have many dates as a high school senior and she somehow managed to thoroughly discourage the boys who showed interest in her. One evening, simply to enjoy themselves and grant themselves a human need to be away from the continual gloom their daughter seemed so determined to cultivate, Georgia's parents left her at home and went to dinner and a show. When they returned she was in bed, sound asleep. Since they knew she was invariably up at such an hour, they went in to ask how she was. When she could not be roused, they immediately rushed into the medicine cabinet and found that a bottle of tranquilizers had been completely emptied. She was rushed to the hospital as a medical emergency and received psychotherapy shortly after she recovered physically. In an instance like this, parents are likely to berate themselves, feeling on some level that, by going out, they abandoned their daughter to die.

On the contrary, had they not been as in touch with her as they were, they might not have known to check the medicine cabinet and respond to the problem situation in a constructive and straightforward manner.

CHAPTER 9

We Seek Our Own Destinies

> May, listen: it does not take nine months, it takes fifty
> years to make a man, fifty years of sacrifice, of will, of
> . . . of so many things!
>
> ANDRÉ MALRAUX
> *(Man's Fate)*

SEVERAL YEARS AGO a major study on adolescent behavior
was conducted by Dr. Daniel Offer and his associates to
determine whether the personality of the adolescent deter-
mines the adult character structure. Did passionately introspective adolescents become loners, poets, and suicides? Did
gregarious extroverts become business successes?

The study followed a relatively large number of youngsters up through adulthood and found that the vast majority turned into normal, well-adjusted adults no matter
how they acted as teenagers. The range of behavior was so
great among them that it was impossible to foretell how they
would turn out or even what constituted abnormal behavior.

The study again tells what a complex and difficult stage
adolescence is. It also tells that virtually every single adolescent whom we have discussed and classified also contains
many strengths that should not be overlooked. The topic of
this book has caused me to focus upon the vulnerabilities,
the conflicts, the emotional deficits within an adolescent and
within his immediate environment. We should not lose sight
of the fact that these weaknesses are usually embedded in
a whole complex personality, one that usually contains many
emotional assets that can be, and should be, built upon.

Too often one becomes so concerned with the problems of a particular adolescent that one loses sight of the bigger picture.

It is likely, for example, that those teenagers in the study we just mentioned developed at their own individual paces. A hypothetical introverted, introspective young man, who never attended or enjoyed social gatherings, may have used his time alone to sort out pressing identity conflicts. Later on, perhaps as a young adult, his introspection, which helped him resolve some major problems, became less predominant. Or, to put it another way, having learned how to examine and deal with his own feelings he may have become more sociable, self-confident, and extroverted in the following years. In the long run, he successfully rounded himself out.

Conversely, our hypothetical extroverted manipulator may in the course of becoming a young adult encounter rejections, challenges he cannot meet, or simply a milieu he becomes disenchanted with. As a result, he might become more reflective and not as shallow and superficially outgoing. He too acquires another dimension of the human personality at a later time. Both boys created and forged their emotional destinies in their own informal ways.

At this stage in our discussion the concerned adult should have acquired some basic new insights into understanding troubled adolescents. By now the reader should have a working knowledge of what adolescence is, the parameters of what can be realistically expected of ourselves and the adolescents around us, the most common pitfalls and mistakes made by well-intentioned, devoted parents. Most important of all is the need an adolescent has for a stable, supportive home environment, one that somehow creates a delicate balance between fortifying a budding sense of autonomy and recognizing true and sensitive areas of dependence.

If there is one overriding point I might add to this in our concluding chapter, it would be the need to help an ado-

lescent seek his own destiny. That is, after all, the underlying aim of adolescence itself. The conflicts these youngsters encounter that lead them to suicide often are due to
the inability an adolescent feels to forge his own destiny.

What follows here are long- and short-term ways in which
a concerned adult can serve as counselor, catalyst, and mid-
wife to this process. I cannot hope to cover all problems
a particular family might encounter. But I have included
a very comprehensive list of reference materials that should
be able to point a family in the direction that happens to
be right for them.

I use the word destiny very deliberately. For destiny
implies a long future life. Those adolescents who choose
religious cults are too confused and overwhelmed by the
task of carving out an adult life. Instead they commit a symbolic sort of suicide and engage in a massive kind of denial
that they ever will grow up by immersing themselves in an
unchanging, static, "timeless" environment.

Unlike, for example, America's early settlers, who also established communal colonies, the cultists do not have an
ultimate destiny, a sense of future, a constellation of ideals
to pursue.

The great preponderance of adolescents do not belong to
cults. But many have enormous difficulties in constructing
a variety of acceptable potential destinies, let alone choosing one that is perfect for them. In some cases perhaps their
expectations are unrealistically and understandably too high.
Life, no matter what one's age, contains moments and days
and perhaps months of frustration, disappointment, emptiness, loneliness, and the mundane rhythms of routine. Life
contains much more than that, of course. An adolescent who
visualizes adult life as a large room that one may somehow
completely design according to personal specifications may
be unprepared to face up maturely to life as it is.

He may expect to be able to create a destiny for himself
that precludes unavoidable, enervating experiences. (Who

would not design a life free from those things if it were humanly possible?)

The ability to create a meaningful destiny, one that permits the adolescent to look forward to the future and take pride in his skills and his potential, is often enough to get him over whatever disturbing conflicts he encounters.

When an adolescent cannot do that at the traditional times, such as the year in which one is supposed to declare one's college major or upon graduation day, adults are often concerned. Most parents are anxious about the future happiness of their children. This is justifiable and natural. Too often, though, expressing that concern becomes an especially heavy burden on a confused youth. This is particularly true of adolescents who announce their intention of taking a year off after graduation or during college. They commonly inform their parents and teachers that they simply are not ready to make a decision that will determine the course of the rest of their lives. They are not willing, at nineteen or at twenty-one, to slip into the harness of the adult nine-to-five jobs, of climbing a career ladder, of establishing a permanent home.

Common as this phenomenon is, many parents react with unnecessary panic. Some feel that the child's temporary abandonment of the customary path toward adulthood will be ongoing. They are afraid that perhaps the child will never develop a skill that will permit him to enjoy a reasonably secure living or raise a family comfortably, that he will wake up several years later only to find that it is too late to do anything about it.

There are a few cases in which this happens. Far more often these adolescents are normal in every respect. They are, in fact, doing something that is indispensable for their long-term adjustment to adulthood. Erik Erikson has labeled the time off a psychosocial moratorium.

What Erikson means is simply that adolescents have to pause for a period of time, to take time off so they can reexamine their values before proceeding with their emotional development, the path that leads to adulthood.

As we have stressed, it is a massive task. To put their houses in order, to ready themselves for the big plunge, to arm themselves emotionally for the rest of their lives they often need to take this temporary break. At this point the reader should be able to recognize that adolescence itself is work, not in the sense of an adult's salary-paying job perhaps, but a Herculean emotional effort. Any adult who has found himself dissatisfied with his career and tried to reevaluate what exactly it is he wants to do knows how difficult making a permanent adjustment is. For an adolescent, who does not have some of the strengths the experience of conducting an adult life provides, it may be far more difficult.

To grasp in some small way how emotionally draining adolescence can be, one simply has to recall one's last vocational or marital crisis. An adolescent often lives with volatile conflicts about career and love for years on end.

In essence, then, there often comes a time when an adolescent has to drop out of the mainstream of competitive society to catch his breath. An adult can be of tremendous help during a crisis of this kind by having implicit faith and confidence in the child's judgment. Anyone who has heard an adolescent in such a situation remarking, "My parents are behind me all the way," knows what a difference it makes in the child's sense of security and belief in himself.

The sheer number of people who have made it from adolescence to functioning, ambitious adulthood should, in itself, be a reassurance. For all their rebelliousness, adolescents are prey to the same pressures of conformity as are adults. Our values and goals have undergone modification throughout the years. In all probability, theirs will too. It does not, for example, take an adolescent dropout long to see that a dead-end job in a large department store is less gratifying than pursuing a professional career in the "obnoxious, insensitive, capitalistic marketplace."

As a psychoanalyst, I do not believe in making value judgments. The purpose of psychoanalysis, in part, is to help someone resolve whatever emotional conflicts he has that prevent him from discovering his true self and pursuing what he really wants to do. There is a major difference between someone who, after receiving a master's degree in sociology, becomes a carpenter because he has always wanted to work with his hands in the open air, and someone else who becomes a carpenter because unconsciously he fears that his becoming a successful businessman will destroy his father. In the first instance, a person is doing what he truly wants to do, perhaps in the face of his parents' opposition, his parents' needs, and what his socioeconomic class expects. In the second instance, the person is doing something that meets nobody's needs.

Some adolescents devote their moratorium period to traveling around the world.

Helen, for example, was a twenty-year-old biology major who had intended to go into research. Suddenly, at the end of her junior year, she decided to spend the money she had accumulated during many summers of waiting on tables and lab technician work to travel through Ireland, England, France, Belgium, Germany, and other countries. Her parents were somewhat aghast at her decision to do nothing for a year. They knew how difficult it was to go back to school once one had left it for an extended period.

Yet Helen was not really doing nothing. While seeing the world she was going over in her mind, in an informal way, exactly how she felt about the career she had intended to choose. Over the months she reviewed her reservations, the limitations of the career as well as its advantages, what she could reasonably expect to produce, and therefore what she could realistically expect from her professional life. By the time she had concluded her travels she decided that she was most interested in genetics. So she returned to school, finished a year and a half late due to the extra courses she wanted to take, and went on to pursue the life she wanted. In a sense, she actually saved time by taking this break. For otherwise she would probably have given in to the pressures to finish up and find an ordinary job.

She would have had to face up painfully to her inevitable dissatisfaction while mired in a job she never wanted in the first place.

Other adolescents choose to do equally "specious" things. These can range from spending a year on a fishing trawler to hiking in the Rockies.

Often they successfully channel their energies in activities that are both idealistic and result oriented. I refer to the social service fields such as VISTA, the Peace Corps, Manpower programs, United Way, among others.

These organizations do not pay a great deal. However, at this stage of development, an adolescent does not want money. What he does get from these experiences is usually much more valuable than a comparatively large income. He gets an opportunity to feel needed, useful, and cared for. He is able to feel that his life has an altruistic meaning and purpose. He also gets valuable exposure to how bureaucracies and their officials operate (which, not incidentally, helps prepare him for what the real world is like).

Above all, he gets the opportunity to feel that he is making decisions for himself. He is getting his first true taste of creating his adult destiny. Parents who worry about such children should be consoled by the knowledge that the Peace Corps may not be the job of a lifetime, but while carrying out his chores, being exposed to other people and other cultures unlike his own, the adolescent is getting in touch with his common humanity. He is experiencing a different environment, which permits him realistically to evaluate his own roots, his own identity. He is able to keep constructively active while wrestling with his identity problems. No matter how far removed the work he performs is from his eventual life's work, chances are very good he has not lost sight of the unresolved questions. No one wants to find a solution more quickly than he does.

These types of experiences cannot help but broaden an adolescent's perspective. They may also serve to save an adolescent's life by removing him from an environment that may be destructive, narrow, and high pressured.

Don was a twenty-year-old college student who found the moratorium particularly important. Don was the son of a dynamic, aggressive physician who was obsessed by the conviction that his son should follow in his footsteps.

Since early childhood, Don was encouraged to choose a career in medicine. From grammar school through high school, his father placed enormous emphasis on Don's academic performance so that he would get into a first-rate college. Nor did the pressure abate during his undergraduate years. Don felt even more pressed as his father's anxiety grew over the fiercely competitive standards for admission to medical schools.

Finally, as a junior, Don could not take it any longer. He had done reasonably well academically but just could not drive himself at the fever pitch his father demanded. Taking a ferocious interest in every course and every examination Don encountered, his father applied a great deal of pressure for him to do especially well on a particularly crucial examination. Don, however, found that particular subject boring and could not throw himself into the fray. As the examination date neared, to add to his dilemma, his best friend moved to another section of the country.

Don felt unprotected and at his father's mercy. His self-esteem dropped and he felt more and more impotent and alienated. It was as though he could see a disaster about to overtake him but simply did not have the energy left to get out of the way.

Two days before the examination took place Don felt that he had no future. To continue under his father's domination was to have no life of his own, to have no destiny except that which his father ordered for him. A career in medicine itself became in his mind nothing more than a totalitarian edict to which he must submit. Rather than seeing a physician's life as providing him with a skill and an income that would guarantee his independence, Don saw becoming a doctor as ultimately crushing any chance he had to acquire self-reliance and autonomy.

Seeing no way out, he attempted to kill himself and thereby provoked a crisis. His father finally relented and permitted him to see a psychoanalyst. Don had wanted to seek help several years before, but his father had forbidden it (prejudice against psychological help is not unknown among doctors), ostensibly because psychoanalysis was unscientific. When his son's life became endangered, the father's attitude changed and his true feelings for resisting psychological help all these years became clearer.

Many lay people are simply unaware of the essential therapeutic reasons that lie behind the confidentiality of the analyst-patient relationship. It is indispensable in establishing trust. It is also necessary to prevent inquiries and outside interference that can intrude sufficiently into the therapeutic relationship so that it will sabotage it.

Don's father knew about the necessity for confidentiality. As though to underscore his need to intrude into his son's life, he demanded Don's analyst provide him with regular reports about his son's progress. The analyst adamantly refused to do so. Although the analyst would have done much the same thing for his other patients as well, in this particular instance it served firmly to break the destructive cycle that had driven Don to receive psychiatric attention in the first place.

His father grudgingly accepted this. As a result, his son received his first experience of being able to relate to an adult when and as he chose to, without coercion and without the worry that the adult would tell him what to do.

As it turned out, Don had a love for medicine. He discovered that because he had been ordered all his life to pursue that career, he really had no way of knowing whether his interest sprang from genuine intellectual curiosity or from a need to please his father. He had never had the experience of making up his mind, absolutely on his own, on major matters concerning his destiny. Naturally, he had grave doubts whether he would ever be capable of doing so.

Beneath all this was his understandable rage against the overwhelming interference he had grown up with and the terror that had accompanied that anger and buried it, the terror that if he stood up to authority he would be totally crushed.

Ultimately, Don decided the only way he would be able to come to terms with himself was to drop out of school temporarily and join the Peace Corps. This moratorium lasted two years. It represented a constructive effort to be on his own, to contribute in a productive way, and, perhaps above all, to be free of external manipulative pressures.

Ironically, upon his return, Don decided that he indeed wanted to become a doctor. He returned to school, completed his senior year with straight A's, and then gained admission to medical school. He finally chose, of all things, to pursue his father's specialty and joined his father's practice.

What is important about this vignette is that, through the moratorium in the Peace Corps, Don had placed himself in a temporary setting that neither limited his future life nor attempted to mold him to its needs. In this environment he was provided the opportunity to sort out his own destiny. Just as important, it was the adult world that was successfully able to handle and support his needs throughout his crisis. It was able to respond in a way that saved his life. The Peace Corps is an adult institution in some ways specifically chartered to channel the immense energy and idealism of youth. Don's physician father also represented the adult world. His parents ultimately stood behind him and were sufficiently flexible to accept his decision to take time off. They too deserve credit.

As with all things concerning individual growth, it is important to remember that no one could have taken ultimate constructive responsibility for changing Don's life but Don. Others could help, but he, as the rest of us, had to do it himself. The type of "therapy" the Peace Corps indirectly provided is also available by way of other activities, such as political campaigns in which, as a recent Democratic party presidential nomination has shown, adolescents play a positive and decisive role.

Any discussion revolving around adolescent suicide, as we have seen, inevitably involves an examination of the primitive ideas of a person's psyche, the powerful and volatile emotional drives that exist just below the surface.

In trying to help an adolescent deal constructively with the primitive side of his nature, which so often proves overwhelming, there is another useful outlet that focuses directly upon it, that is, creative endeavors such as painting, poetry, sculpture, photography, music, dance, and other artistic activities.

As Freud pointed out, art is a means by which a person is able to get in touch with hidden parts of himself and make them into something coherent, constructive, and pleasing. The act of self-expression itself can bring great emotional relief to an adolescent.

Encouraging adolescents to pursue creative endeavors can help them receive and enjoy emotional rewards they might otherwise miss. As performers, for example, they benefit in many ways. Adolescents are by necessity in a highly self-involved period of life. Performing is a positive and socially accepted way to stand out in a crowd, to get a reassuring sense of one's uniqueness, and to weave a soothing web of "competence" around themselves. When creating they are permitted, and ideally encouraged, to take their pressing conflicts, wounds, and hopes very seriously. Their concerns are elevated to the raw material of art. As an idealistic activity that by its nature seems to dismiss the routine and mundane considerations of earning a living, performing offers a welcome sanctuary from the outside world, a career one can form to one's own specifications, at least in theory. Through it, in short, an adolescent can receive the hope that he can create his own very special adult destiny.

The more deeply an adolescent immerses himself in art, the more he normally is spurred on to seek out positive role models in his chosen field. He often chooses to find out as much as he can about a particular creative world, and this brings him into contact with many other youngsters and adults who have the same interests. It expands his emotional and intellectual vistas as well.

If his drive is strong enough, the urge to succeed as a creative artist may be enough to make him look forward with a hopeful attitude toward the future. It can help steel him against all the ambivalence and fears about succeeding as an adult that he would otherwise have to face feeling defenseless, overwhelmed, and without resources or solace.

Much as we recognize and appreciate the value of art in its own right, it is important to stress that our purpose here is to demonstrate the important emotionally therapeutic rewards it can provide. Sometimes creative work can also provide the means by which adolescents can comfortably fulfill other basic identity needs, which would otherwise be unmet.

Take for example an adolescent who has trouble making friends. Perhaps he finds it nearly impossible to attend high school dances. The feelings of being awkward, unattractive, unpopular, and worthless under those conditions just prove too much. He has created a vicious, self-defeating cycle for himself.

Suppose this youth has some literary ability and is somehow encouraged to join the high school literary magazine.

This same youth, his dignity preserved, might have very little trouble, or no trouble at all, attending after-school meetings and socializing with his fellow staff members far into the night. He is doing it all, in his own mind, of course, for art. But if in practice his emotional needs are being fulfilled and he learns how to be more comfortable with people, it makes absolutely no difference how he presents his reality to himself.

Though he may be miserable standing against a wall while a "ladies' choice" is announced, he will be comfortable attending all-night editorial meetings with these same girls, or storming angrily into a principal's office to protest unwarranted censorship of the magazine.

Creative activities can be the means through which an adolescent learns to stand up for himself, learns how to negotiate conflicts, and becomes deeply involved and immersed in the world around him. They are a way of indirectly receiving important approval from those around him, those he wants to please and impress the most. The degree to which acting or metalwork or photography becomes an adolescent's "specialty" may be the degree to which he feels he has a unique place in the world, a place worth cultivating. Since artistic expression is also a means of channeling one's more "primitive" emotions and drives, participating in virtually any form of artistic expression may be an ideal way to bring the demands of one's inner world into synchrony with the demands of the surrounding world.

What about those adolescents who need direct and immediate intervention? There are a variety of treatment facilities available (see Appendices). Perhaps the most often utilized form of treatment is supportive psychotherapy. It involves a series of meetings between physician and patient in which the therapist, through reassurance, encouragement, suggestion, and persuasion, attempts to help the adolescent gain emotional equilibrium.

No small part of the immense gratification that working with deeply troubled adolescents offers, to both the professional and the layman, comes from the enormous vitality and potential they possess alongside their turmoil.

The places where change can come from are various. Parents grow over the years just as their children do. The experience of living, the experience of raising children often spurs adults themselves into greater maturity, sophistication, insight, and tolerance. The young, without realizing it, often help their elders grow, enabling their parents to provide a much more supportive environment.

An adolescent's life circumstances can also change, bringing about profound and remarkable improvements. He may discover that he has a fascination for the law, for the sciences, or for the arts. The successes he enjoys in these areas may themselves be therapeutic. Experiencing a successful love relationship, getting out in the world, and enjoying the pleasures of independence and self-reliance and accomplishment often work wonders.

Medical students, to cite the first example that comes to mind, often find their marriages flounder during the course of their perhaps overly vigorous training. They are often unable to spend significant amounts of time at home during the day or night. As though the feelings of stress and alienation are physically communicable, wives often have a difficult time becoming pregnant.

Upon completing their training, establishing a practice, and resuming relatively normal and stable work schedules, the young doctor and his wife find these problems seem to clear up quickly and a family soon follows.

The psychoanalytic philosophy contains some important lessons for those involved with troubled adolescents. It teaches us that an adolescent's attitudes and behavior (as well as our own) are the results of forces within the mind that are beyond our conscious control. It also teaches us to try to understand why an adolescent is acting as he does rather than to pass judgment on him. The more open and receptive an adult is to this way of relating, the more an adolescent will be understood, which is the first step toward providing crucial support and help.

If the adult is willing to examine his feelings and attitudes, the more likely he stimulates a similar attitude in his children. Adolescents usually want desperately to transcend the threatening and destructive types of confusion they have about themselves. As I noted earlier, the first important step toward resolving a problem is having the courage to admit that one exists, and the more basic the problem is, the more threatening this admission. This implies, however, that the more courage and determination and resolve a person brings to these problems, the greater the rewards will be.

Paradoxical as it might seem at first, the more frightening an emotional problem is, the more important it proves to be and the greater the benefits will be of ultimately addressing it. Outside help, as we have seen, is available in many forms. It is hoped that the majority of people in our society are no longer as confused and frightened by the mental health sciences as they once were. As the tangible benefits of the forms of help I have discussed become universally known, more people will be able to overcome the skewed and destructive concept of self-reliance satirized by novelist Kurt Vonnegut when he wrote, "This is the United States of America, where nobody has the right to rely on anybody else."

The struggle to live and the struggle for independence are parallel processes. Adolescence is a time in which a child is transformed into an adult, a time in which dependency is exchanged for autonomy. We are all mixtures of self-reliance and autonomy.

Some philosophers maintain that the universe is a duality that consists of creative and destructive elements, of life and death. Adolescents plagued by suicidal thoughts and experiences also represent a profound and very moving duality.

To explore with them the sources of the wasteland they sense within and around them is also a way of discovering the altruism and the high hopes that have often made their despair so overwhelming in the first place.

For it is adolescence, perhaps more than any other age group, that is obsessed with trying to find out what is worthless and false and what is meaningful and worthwhile. Most of us to one degree or another set our sights on survival, trying to enjoy what gratifications we can in passing. Survival is challenging enough, and we often carve out the most secure niche we can for ourselves and settle for that.

Adolescents, for all their vulnerability, strive for more than that. Like Icarus', their fall often comes from flying too near the sun.

They need to draw upon our strength, our patience, our resilience, and our compassion. Our relationship with them can become the most certain method we have of averting the irreparable and needless loss of young life. It is also the best means to test and reevaluate our values and our way of life. When we help adolescents achieve adulthood they can challenge us to acquire greater maturity, integrity, and insight into the meaning of our own lives.

Appendices

RECOMMENDED READINGS

Amir, M. "Suicide among Minors in Israel." *Israel Annals of Psychiatry* 11 (1973):219–67.

Asuni, T. "Attempted Suicide in Western Nigeria." *West African Medical Journal* 16 (1967):51–54.

Bakwin, H. "Suicide in Children and Adolescents." *Journal of Pediatrics* 50 (1957):749–69.

Balser, B. H., and Masterson, J. F. "Suicide in Adolescents." *American Journal of Psychiatry* 116 (1959):400–404.

Barter, J. T., Swaback, D. O., and Todd, D. "Adolescent Suicide Attempts: A Follow-up Study of Hospitalized Patients." *Archives of General Psychiatry* 19 (1968):523–27.

Bergstrand, C. G., and Otto, Ulf. "Suicidal Attempts in Adolescence and Childhood." *Acta Pediatricia Scandinavia* 51 (1962): 17–26.

Bourne, P. G. "Suicide among the Chinese in San Francisco." *American Journal of Public Health* 63 (1973):744–50.

Burstein, A. G., Adams, R. L., and Giffen, M. B. "Assessment of Suicidal Risk by Psychology and Psychiatry Trainees." *Archives of General Psychiatry* 29 (1973):792–93.

Burvill, P. W., McCall, M. G., Reid, T. A., and Stenhouse, N. S. "Methods of Suicide of English and Welch Immigrants in Australia." *British Journal of Psychiatry* 123 (1973):285–94.

* Choron, J. *Suicide*. New York: Charles Scribner's Sons, 1972.

* Coleman, James C. *Abnormal Psychology in Modern Life*. Glenview, Ill.: Scott Foresman and Company, 1976.

Connell, H. M. "Attempted Suicide in School Children." *The Medical Journal of Australia* 1 (1972):686–90.

Dizmang, L. H., Watson, J., May, P. A., and Bopp, J. "Adolescent Suicide at an Indian Reservation." *American Journal of Orthopsychiatry* 44 (1974):43–49.

Dorpat, T. L., et al. "Broken Homes and Attempted and Completed Suicide." *Archives of General Psychiatry* 12 (1965): 213–16.

* Especially recommended for a comprehensive coverage of adolescent suicide in nontechnical terms.

Drye, R. C., Goulding, R. L., and Goulding, M. E. "No Suicide Decisions, Patient Monitoring of Suicidal Risks." *American Journal of Psychiatry* 130 (1973):171–74.

* Erikson, E. H. *Childhood and Society.* New York: W. W. Norton & Company, Inc., 1950.

Faigel, H. C. "Suicide among Young Persons." *Clinical Pediatrics* 5 (1966):187–90.

* Farnsworth, Dana. *Mental Health in College and University.* Cambridge: Harvard University Press, 1957.

* Finch, S. M., and Poznanski, E. O. *Adolescent Suicide.* Springfield, Ill.: Charles C Thomas, 1971.

Gould, Robert E. "Suicide Problems in Children and Adolescents." *American Journal of Psychotherapy* 19 (1965):228–46.

Greer, S. "The Relationships between Parental Loss and Attempted Suicide: A Control Study." *British Journal of Psychiatry* 110 (1964):698–705.

Hendin, H. "Student Suicide: Death as a Life Style." *Journal of Nervous and Mental Diseases* 160 (1975):204–219.

Kestenbaum, R. "Time and Death in Adolescence." In H. Feifel, ed. *The Meaning of Death.* New York: McGraw-Hill, 1959, pp. 99–113.

Liebermann, L. P. "Three Cases of Attempted Suicide in Children." *British Journal of Medical Psychology* 26 (1953): 110–14.

Lindemann, Eric. "Symptomatology and Management of Acute Grief." *American Journal of Psychiatry* 101 (1944):7–21.

Maltzberger, J. T., and Buie, D. H. "Countertransference Hate in the Treatment of Suicidal Patients." *Archives of General Psychiatry* 30 (1974):625–33.

Margolin, N. L., and Teicher, J. D. "Thirteen Adolescent Male Suicide Attempts: Dynamic Considerations." *Journal of the American Academy of Child Psychiatry* 7 (1968):296–315.

Mattson, A., Seese, L. R., and Hawkins, J. W. "Suicidal Behavior as a Child Psychiatric Emergency: Clinical Characteristics and Follow-up Results." *Archives of General Psychiatry* 20 (1969):100–109.

Miller, J. P. "Suicide in Adolescence." *Adolescence* 10 (1975):11–24.

Moss, L. M., and Hamilton, D. M. "The Psychotherapy of the Suicidal Patient." *American Journal of Psychiatry* 112 (1956):8810–820.

Sabbath, Joseph C. "The Suicidal Adolescent—The Expendable Child." *Journal of the American Academy of Child Psychiatry* 8 (1969):272–89.

Schecter, M. "The Recognition and Treatment of Suicide in Children." In G. Scheidman and N. Farberow, eds. *Clues to Suicide*. New York: Blakiston Division, McGraw-Hill, 1957, pp. 131–42.

Schneidman, E. S. "Suicide among Adolescents." *California School Health* 2 (1966):1–4.

Shaw, C. R., and Schelkun, R. F. "Suicidal Behavior in Children." *Psychiatry* 28 (1965):157–68.

Stanley, E. J., and Barter, J. T. "Adolescent Suicidal Behavior." *American Journal of Orthopsychiatry* 40 (1970):87–96.

Steba, E. "The Schoolboy Suicide in Andre Gide's Novel *The Counterfeiters*." *American Imago* 8 (1951):307–320.

Tabachnick, N. "Creative Suicidal Crises." *Archives of General Psychiatry* 29 (1973):258–63.

* Teicher, J. D. "A Solution to the Chronic Problem of Living: Adolescent Attempted Suicide." In J. C. Schoolar, ed. *Current Issues in Adolescent Psychiatry*. New York: Brunner/Mazel, 1973, pp. 129–47.

Wieder, H., and Kaplan, E. H. "Drug Use in Adolescents: Psychodynamic Meaning and Pharmacogenic Effect." *Psychoanalytic Study of the Child* 24 (1969):339–431.

Zilboorg, G. "Considerations on Suicide, with Particular Reference to That of the Young." *American Journal of Orthopsychiatry* 7 (1937):15–31.

One of the first studies on suicide which still contains valuable insights is:

Durkheim, E. *Suicide*. Glencoe, Ill.: Free Press, 1952.
Also see:
Feinstein, S., and Giovacchini, P., eds. *Adolescent Psychiatry*. Vol. 1–8. Chicago: University of Chicago Press, 1968–80.

INSTITUTIONAL RESOURCES

The establishment of relevant institutions indicates that our society is well aware of the enormity of the problem of adolescent suicide. There are, today, many facilities designed to help youth in distress.

The following agencies and institutions are found in most cities, villages, and suburbs throughout the United States.

Family service agencies. Most of these are community sponsored and have social workers on their staff. They also have at least one psychiatrist who is used as a consultant.

Some such agencies are denominational, such as the Jewish Children's Bureau and Catholic Charities. Lutherans also support hospitals that provide services similar to those offered by these agencies.

Juvenile courts.

Juvenile protection agencies.

Hospitals. All hospitals connected with medical schools, as well as other hospitals that have more than two hundred beds, have a social-work department and department of psychiatry. This means that adolescents who represent a suicidal risk can be treated either as in-patients or out-patients.

Hot lines. Many cities and most college campuses have a telephone service that can offer an immediate contact for disturbed youth and attempt to direct them to seek appropriate help. These numbers are easily available in the local directories, or they can be obtained from any police station.

Specific information regarding services in any particular locale can be obtained by writing to:

Leo H. Berman, M.D.
Psychiatric Institute of America
1010 Wisconsin Avenue, N.W.
Washington, D.C. 20007

SUICIDE PREVENTION AND CRISIS INTERVENTION AGENCIES IN THE UNITED STATES

Alabama

* Crisis Center of Jefferson
   County, Inc.
3600 Eighth Avenue South
Birmingham 35222
Director: Edward B. Speaker
Emergency: (205) 323-7777
Business: (same)

North Central Alabama Crisis
   Call Center
304 Fourth Avenue S.E.
Decatur 35601
Director: Raymond C. McCaslin
Emergency: (205) 355-8000
Business: (205) 355-8505

* Member of the American Association of Suicidology as of June 1980.

Muscle Shoals Mental Health
Center
635 West College Street
Florence 35630
Director: Thomas Pirkle
Emergency: (205) 764-3431
Business: (same)

Alaska

* Suicide Prevention and
Crisis Center
P.O. Box 2863
Anchorage 99501
President: James A. Smith, Jr.
Emergency: (907) 279-3214
Business: (907) 277-0027

Arizona

Mental Health Services Suicide
Prevention Center
1825 East Roosevelt
Phoenix 85006
Chief: James E. Matters
Emergency: (602) 258-6301
Business: (602) 258-6381

* Suicide Prevention/Crisis
Center
801 South Prudence Road
Tucson 85710
Director: Jim Tillema
Emergency: (602) 795-0123
Business: (same)

Information and Referral
Service
2302 East Speedway, Suite 210
Tucson 85719
Director: Kathy Woolpert
Emergency: (602) 323-1303
Business: (same)

California

Marilyn Adams Suicide
Prevention Center of
Bakersfield, Inc.
800 Eleventh Street
Bakersfield 93304
Executive Secretary: Sylvia
Prestige
Emergency: (805) 325-1232
Business: None

Suicide Prevention of
Santa Cruz County, Inc.
P.O. Box 36
Ben Lomond 95005
Director: Rev. Warren Howell
Emergency: (408) 426-2342
Business: (408) 688-1111

Suicide Prevention of Alameda
County, Inc.
P.O. Box 9102
Berkeley 94709
Director: Dr. Ronald Tauber
Emergency: (415) 849-2212
(415) 537-1323
Business: (415) 848-1515
(415) 573-1324

* Suicide Prevention and Crisis
Center of San Mateo County
1811 Trousdale Drive
Burlingame 94010
Director: Charlotte Ross
Emergency: (415) 877-5600
(415) 367-8000
(415) 726-5581
Business: (415) 877-5604

* Monterey County Suicide
  Prevention Center
P.O. Box 3241
Carmel 93921
Director: Elizabeth Corr
Emergency: (408) 375-6966
Business: (same)

Help Line, Inc.
P.O. Box 5658
China Lake 93555
Director: Joe McIntire
Emergency: (714) 446-5531
Business: (same)

* Suicide Prevention of
  Yolo County
618 Sunset Court
Davis 95616
Director: Patricia Allen
Emergency: (916) 758-1461
Business: (same)

Crisis House
126 West Main Street
El Cajon 92021
Director: James Keeley
Emergency: (714) 444-1194
Business (same)

Saddleback Valley "Help Line"
P.O. Box 436
El Toro 92630
President: Robert Adams
Emergency: (714) 830-2522
Business: (same)

Help in Emotional Trouble
P.O. Box 468
Fresno 93721
Director: Caryl Gill
Emergency: (805) 485-1432
Business: (805) 264-0386

Hot Line—Garden Grove
c/o Garden Grove Counseling
  Service
12345 Euclid Street
Garden Grove 92640
Director: Dr. Glen H.
  McCormick
Emergency: (714) 636-2424
Business: (714) 636-1060

New Hope 24-Hour Counseling
  Service
12141 Lewis Street
Garden Grove 92640
Director: Dr. Raymond E.
  Beckering
Emergency: (213) 639-4673
Business: (213) 534-0275

"Help Now" Line
2750 Bellflower Blvd., Suite 204
Long Beach 90815
Directors: Robert F. Gunter
           Tom Stockton
Emergency: (213) 435-7669
Business: (213) 595-2353
             (213) 595-2354

Help Line Contact Clinic
427 West Fifth Street, Suite 500
Los Angeles 90013
Directors: Lloyd T. Workman
           Clyde Reynolds
           J. David Gray
Emergency: (213) 620-0144
Business: (213) 620-0148

Los Angeles Free Clinic
115 North Fairfax
Los Angeles 90036
Director: Mark Edelstein
Emergency: (213) 935-9669
Business: (213) 938-9141

† Suicide Prevention Center
1041 South Menlo Avenue
Los Angeles 90006
Director: Sam M. Heilig
Emergency: (213) 386-5111
Business: (same)

North Bay Suicide
  Prevention, Inc.
P.O. Box 2444
Napa 94558
Director: Susan Thomas
Emergency: (707) 643-2555
              (707) 255-2555
              (707) 963-2555

Suicide Prevention and Crisis
  Intervention Center
101 South Manchester Avenue
Orange 92668
Director: Dr. Carlos
  Munoz-Mellowes
Emergency: (714) 633-9393
Business: (same)

Suicide Crisis Intervention
  Center
c/o Palm Springs Mental
  Health Clinic
1720 East Vista Chino
Palm Springs 92262
Coordinator: Georgia Winkler
Emergency: (714) 346-9502
Business: (714) 327-8426

Pasadena Mental Health
  Association
1815 North Fair Oaks
Pasadena 91103
Administrator: Dr. Malcolm
  Coffee
Emergency: (213) 798-0907
Business: (213) 681-1381

Psychiatric Crisis Clinic
Sacramento Medical Center
  Emergency Area
2315 Stockton Blvd.
Sacramento 95817
Chief: Dr. Richard Yarvis
Emergency: (916) 454-5707
Business: (same)

* Suicide Prevention Service
  of Sacramento County, Inc.
P.O. Box 449
Sacramento 95802
Director: Michael Chiechi
Emergency: (916) 441-1138
Business: (same)

Marin Suicide Prevention
  Center
P.O. Box 792
San Anselmo 94960
Director: Dr. Richard Reubin
Emergency: (415) 454-4524
Business: (415) 454-4525

Suicide Prevention Service
1999 North "D" Street
San Bernadino 92405
Director: Phyllis Plate
Emergency: (714) 886-4880
Business: (714) 882-4510

† Member certified by the AAS as having approved suicide prevention and crisis intervention programs as of June 1980.

* DEFY Counseling Line
2870 Fourth Avenue
San Diego 92103
Director: Drew E. Leavens
Emergency: (714) 236-3339
Business: (same)

Help Center
5069 College Avenue
San Diego 92115
Emergency: (714) 582-HELP
Business: (714) 582-4442

Suicide Prevention, Inc.
307 Twelfth Avenue
San Francisco 94118
Director: Roger Cornut
Emergency: (415) 221-1424
Business: (415) 752-4866

Center for Special Problems
2107 Van Ness Avenue
San Francisco 94109
Director: Dr. Eugene Turrell
Emergency: (415) 558-4801
Business: (same)

Suicide and Crisis Service
2221 Enborg Lane
San Jose 95128
Coordinator: Mark Antonucci,
  Ph.D.
Emergency: (408) 279-6250
Business: (same)

North Bay Suicide Prevention
401 Amador Street
Vallejo 94590
President: Susan Thomas
Emergency: (707) 643-2555
Business: None

Suicide Prevention Service
c/o Mental Health Association
33 Chrisman
Ventura 93003
Director: Dr. Andrew Morrison
Emergency: (805) 648-2444
Business: (805) 648-5071

Suicide Prevention-Crisis
  Intervention
P.O. Box 4852
Walnut Creek 94596
Director: Philip Lang
Emergency: (415) 939-3232
Business: (415) 939-1916

Colorado

Arapahoe Mental Health
  Center
551 Lansing
Aurora 80010
Director: Dr. Thomas Nelson
Emergency: (303) 761-0620
Business: (same)

Suicide Referral Service
P.O. Box 4438
Colorado Springs 80930
Director: Kenneth W. Felts
Emergency: (303) 471-4357
Business: None

Emergency Psychiatric Service
Colorado General Hospital
4200 East Ninth Avenue
Denver 80220
Director: Mark W. Rhine
Emergency: (303) 394-8297
Business: None

Emergency Room Psychiatric
  Services
Denver General Hospital
West Eighth Avenue & Bannock
Denver 80206
Director: Glenn Swank
Emergency: (303) 244-6835
Business: (303) 893-7001

Suicide and Crisis Control
2459 South Ash
Denver 80222
Director: Rev. Bill Anderson
Emergency: (303) 746-8485
Business: (same)

Crisis Center and Suicide
  Prevention Service
599 Thirty Road
Grand Junction 81501
Director: Don G. Sperber
Emergency: (303) 242-0577
Business: (same)

* Pueblo Suicide Prevention
  Center, Inc.
229 Colorado Avenue
Pueblo 81004
Director: Eleanor Hamm
Emergency: (303) 545-2477
Business: (same)

Connecticut

The Wheeler Clinic, Inc.
  Emergency Services
91 Northwest Drive
Plainsville 06062
Director: Robert P. DeCarli,
  M.A.
Emergency: (203) 747-6801
Business: (same)

Delaware

Psychiatric Emergency
  Telephone Service
Sussex County Community
  Mental Health Center
Beebe Hospital of Sussex
  County
Lewes 19958
Director: Dr. Lion DeBernard
Emergency: (302) 856-6626
Business: (302) 856-6108

Psychiatric Emergency Service
2001 North Dupont Parkway,
  Farnburst
New Castle 19720
Director: Dr. Aydin Z. Bill
Emergency: (302) 656-4428
Business: (302) 654-5121

District of Columbia

American University Multiple
  Emergency Center
Mary Graydon Center,
  Room 316
Washington, D.C. 20016
Directors: Dr. Alan Berman
           Dr. Barry McCarthy
Emergency: (202) 966-9511
Business: (202) 966-9513

Suicide Prevention and
  Emergency Mental Health
  Service
801 North Capitol Street, N.E.
Washington, D.C. 20002
Director: Phyllis Clemmons
Emergency: (202) 629-5222
Business: (202) 347-7041

Florida

† Alachua County Crisis Center
606 S.W. Third Avenue
Gainesville 32601
Director: Elizabeth Jones
Emergency: (904) 375-4636
Business: (same)

† Central Crisis Center of
  · Jacksonville, Inc.
P.O. Box 6393
Jacksonville 32205
Director: Bonnie Jacob
Emergency: (904) 387-5641
Business: (same)

Personal Crisis Service
30 S.E. Eighth Street
Miami 33131
Director: Nina Poschlevaite
Emergency: (305) 379-2611
Business: (305) 379-3642

* We Care, Inc.
112 Pasadena Place
Orlando 32803
Coordinator: Kathy Anderson
Emergency: (305) 425-2624
Business: (same)

Rockledge Crisis and Suicide
  Intervention Service
Brevard County Mental Health
  Center
1770 Cedar Street
Rockledge 32955
Director: Harold E. Frank
Emergency: (305) 784-2433
Business: (305) 632-9480

Crisis Intervention of Sarasota
1650 South Osprey Avenue
Sarasota 33578
Director: Jane Barry
Emergency: (813) 959-6686
Business: None

Adult Mental Health Clinic
Pinellas County
630 Sixth Avenue South
St. Petersburg 33711
Director: Edward Meares
Emergency: (813) 347-0392
Business: (813) 347-2108

* Suicide and Crisis Center of
  Tampa
2214 East Henry Avenue
Tampa 33610
Director: Carlos A. Perez
Emergency: (813) 238-8411
Business: (same)

Crisis Line
707 Chillingworth Drive
West Palm Beach 33401
Director: Robert K. Alsofrom,
  Ph.D.
Emergency: (305) 848-8686
Business: (305) 399-2244

Georgia

Fulton County Emergency
  Mental Health Service
99 Butler Street, S.E.
Atlanta 30303
Director: Richard Lyles, Ph.D.
Emergency: (404) 572-2626
Business: (same)

DeKalb Emergency and Crisis
Intervention Services
Central DeKalb Mental Health
Center
500 Winn Way
Decatur 30030
Director: Jane Yates, R.N.,
M.N.
Emergency: (404) 292-1137
Business: (404) 202-5231

Illinois

* Call for Help—Suicide and
Crisis Intervention Services,
Inc.
7623 West Main
Belleville 62223
Director: Sr. Jo Ann Pisel
Emergency: (618) 397-0968
Business: (same)

Carroll Crisis Intervention
Center
201 Presbyterian Avenue
Carrollton 30117
Director: Stephen B. Blanchette
Emergency: (404) 834-3326
Business: (404) 834-3327

Champaign County Suicide
Prevention and Crisis Service
1206 South Randolph
Champaign 61820
Director: Betty Lazarus
Emergency: (217) 359-4141
Business: (217) 352-7921

Help Line
1512 Bull Street
Savannah 31401
Director: Dr. Daniel Johnston
Emergency: (912) 232-3383
Business: (912) 233-0416

Crisis Intervention Program
4200 North Oak Park Avenue
Chicago 60634
Director: Helen Sunukjian,
Ph.D.
Emergency: (312) 794-3609
Business: (312) 794-4230

Hawaii

* Suicide and Crisis Center of
Volunteer Information and
Referral Service
200 North Vineyard Boulevard
Room 603
Honolulu 96817
Director: Jean A. Lee
Emergency: (808) 536-7234
Business: (same)

Crisis Counseling Service
Jefferson County Mental
Health Center
1300 Salem Road
Mt. Vernon 62864
Director: James L. Nicholson,
M.S.
Emergency: (618) 242-1511
Business: (618) 242-1510

Call for Help
320 East Armstrong Avenue
Peoria 61603
Director: Mrs. Barbara Runyan
Emergency: (309) 691-7373
Business: (309) 673-6481
                    ext. 21

Suicide Prevention Service
520 South Fourth Street
Quincey 62301
Director: Robert Scott, ACSW
Emergency: (217) 222-1166
Business: (217) 223-0413

Open Line Service
114 East Cherry Street
Watseka 60970
Director: Anthony Flore, M.S.
Emergency: (815) 432-5111
Business: (815) 432-5241

Indiana

Suicide Prevention Service—
  Marion County Assoc. for
  Mental Health
1433 North Meridian Street
Indianapolis 46202
Director: Patricia C. Jones
Emergency: (317) 632-7575
Business: (317) 636-2491

* Suicide Prevention of St.
  Joseph County
532 South Michigan Street
South Bend 46601
Director: Bert Harrison
Emergency: (219) 288-4842
Business: (same)

Iowa

Lee County Mental Health
  Center
110 North Eighth Street
Keokuk 52632
Director: Harry D. Harper,
  M.D.
Emergency: (319) 524-3873
Business: (same)

Kansas

Area Mental Health Center
156 Gardendale
Garden City 67846
Director: Harry C. Lester,
  ACSW
Emergency: (316) 276-7689
Business: (same)

Suicide Prevention Center
250 North Seventeenth
Kansas City 66102
Director: Dr. Natalie Hill
Emergency: (913) 371-7171
Business: (913) 371-5707

Can Help
P.O. Box 4253
Topeka 66604
Director: Mrs. Joy Williams
Emergency: (913) 235-3434
Business: (913) 232-0437

Suicide Prevention Service
1045 North Minneapolis
Wichita 67214
Director: Clinton Willsie
Emergency: (316) 268-8251
Business: (same)

Louisiana

† Baton Rouge Crisis
  Intervention Center, Inc.
Student Health Service, LSU
Baton Rouge 70803
Director: Myron C. Mohr,
  Ph.D.
Emergency: (504) 344-0319
Business: (same)

* Crisis Line
1528 Jackson Avenue
New Orleans 70130
Director: Rick Wagner
Emergency: (504) 523-4146
Business: (same)

Maine

Dial Help
The Counseling Center
43 Illinois Avenue
Bangor 04401
Director: Larry Friesen, Ph.D.
Emergency: (207) 947-0366
Business: (same)

Bath-Brunswick Area Rescue,
  Inc.
P.O. Box 534
Brunswick 04011
President: Grant D. Kirker, Jr.
Emergency: (207) 729-4168
Business: (same)

Rescue, Incorporated
331 Cumberland Avenue
Portland 04101
Director: Rev. Arthur Moore
Emergency: (207) 774-2767
Business: (207) 774-4761

Maryland

Crisis Intervention and
  Problem Solving Clinic of
  Sinai Hospital of Baltimore,
  Inc.
Belvedere Avenue at
  Greenspring
Baltimore 21215
Director: Huell E. Connor, Jr.,
  M.D.
Emergency: (301) 367-7800
Business: (same) ext. 8855
                      ext. 8846

Massachusetts

Rescue, Inc.
115 Southampton Street
Boston 02118
Director: Rev. Kenneth B.
  Murphy
Emergency: (617) 426-6600
Business: (617) 442-8000

* The Samaritans
802 Boylston Street
Boston 02199
Director: Shirley Karnovsky
Emergency: (617) 536-2460
Business: (same)

Michigan

Call Someone Concerned
760 Riverside
Adrian 49221
Director: Patricia E. Wentz,
  M.D.
Emergency: (313) 263-6737
Business: (313) 263-2930

Community Service Center—
  Chelsea
775 South Main Street
Chelsea 48118
Director: Mrs. Lucy Howard
Emergency: (313) 475-2676
Business: (same)

† Suicide Prevention and Drug
  Information Center
1151 Taylor Avenue
Detroit 48202
Director: Bruce L. Danto, M.D.
Emergency: (313) 875-5466
Business: (same)

Suicide Prevention Crisis
  Intervention Service
Community Mental Health
  Clinic
Ottawa County Building
Room 114
Grand Haven 49417
Director: James McDowall,
  ACSW
Emergency: (616) 842-4357
Business: (616) 842-5350

Ottawa County Crisis
  Intervention Service
549 West Eighteenth Street
Holland 49423
Program Coordinator:
  David Dewar
Emergency: (313) 392-7045
Business: (same)

Lapeer County Community
  Mental Health Center
1575 Suncrest Drive
Lapeer 48446
Director: Richard I. Berman,
  D.S.W.
Emergency: (313) 664-5959
Business: (same)

Downriver Guidance Clinic
Community Crisis Center
1619 Fort Street
Lincoln Park 48146
Director: Jean Haslett, M.S.W.
Emergency: (313) 383-9000
Business: (313) 388-4630
                  ext. 250

Crisis Center
29200 Hoover Road
Warren 48093
Director: Christopher Murphy
Emergency: (313) 758-6860
Business: (same)

Ypsilanti Area Community
  Services
1637 Holmes Road
Ypsilanti 48197
Director: Sr. Sheila Hedegard
Emergency: (616) 485-0440
Business: (same)

Minnesota

*Contact Twin Cities
83 South Twelfth Street
Minneapolis 55102
Director: Elaine H. Reid
Emergency: (612) 341-2212
Business: (same)

Crisis Intervention Center
Hennepin County General
  Hospital
Minneapolis 55415
Director: Zigfrieds T.
  Stelmachers
Emergency: (612) 330-7777
                  330-7780
Business: (612) 330-7950

Emergency Social Service
413 Auditorium Street
St. Paul 55102
Director: Mrs. Elizabeth K.
  Undis
Emergency: (612) 225-1515
Business: (612) 224-4981
                   451-2718

Mississippi

Listening Post
P.O. Box 2072
Meridian 39301
Director: C. Richard Bahr
Emergency: (601) 693-1001
Business: (same)

Missouri

St. Francis Community Mental
  Health Center
825 Goodhope
Cape Girardeau 63701
Director: Dale Rauh
Emergency: (314) 334-6400

Western Missouri Mental
  Health Center
Suicide Prevention Center
600 East Twenty-Second Street
Kansas City 64108
Director: Nicola Katf, M.D.
Emergency: None
Business: (816) 471-3000

Crisis Intervention, Inc.
P.O. Box 582
Joplin 64801
Director: Mrs. Jack Carter
Emergency: (417) 781-2255
Business: (same)

St. Joseph Suicide Prevention
  Service
St. Joseph State Hospital
St. Joseph 64501
Director: Deward A. Moore
Emergency: (816) 232-1655
Business: (816) 232-8431

* Life Crisis Services, Inc.
7438 Forsyth
Suite 210
St. Louis 63105
Director: Mrs. Gwyn Harvey
Emergency: (314) 721-4310
Business: (same)

Montana

Blackfeet Crisis Center
Blackfeet Reservation
Browning 59417
Director: Audra M. Pambrun
Emergency: (406) 338-5525
                   226-4291
Business: (406) 338-5525

Great Falls Crisis Center
P.O. Box 124
Great Falls 59401
Director: John Breedon
Emergency: (406) 453-6511
Business: (same)

Nebraska

Personal Crisis Service, Inc.
4102 Woolworth
Omaha 68105
Director: B. Wheeler
Emergency: (402) 444-7442
Business: (same)

Nevada

Suicide Prevention and Crisis
  Call Center
Room 206 Mack SS Building
University of Nevada
Reno 89507
Director: James Mikawa
Emergency: (702) 323-6111
Business: (702) 322-8621

New Hampshire

North County Community
  Services, Inc.
227 Main Street
Berlin 03570
Director: Jack Melton
Emergency: (603) 752-7404
Business: (603) 752-4431

* Central New Hampshire
  Community Health Services,
  Inc.
5 Market Lane
Concord 03301
Director: James O. Wells,
  Ph.D.
Emergency: (603) 228-1551
Business: (same)

Intake and Emergency Services
787 Central Avenue
Dover 03820
Director: Jacquelyn Felix
Emergency: (603) 742-0630
Business: (same)

Mental Health Center for
  Southern New Hampshire
4 North Main Street
Salem 03079
Director: Robert Lehmann
Emergency: (603) 898-5936
Business: (same)

New Jersey

Ancora Suicide Prevention
  Service
Ancora Psychiatric Hospital
Hammonton 08037
Director: Leo L. Sell, M.D.
Emergency: (201) 561-1234
Business: (201) 561-1700

Middlesex County-Crisis
  Intervention
37 Oakwood Avenue
Metuchen 08840
Director: Doulat Keswani, M.D.
Emergency: (201) 549-6000

* Screening-Crisis Intervention
  Program
1129B Woodlane Road
Mt. Holly 08060
Director: H. Dillon Crager
Emergency: (609) 764-1100
Business: (609) 267-1377

Crisis, Referral and Information
232 East Front Street
Plainfield 07060
Director: Donald Fell
Emergency: (201) 561-4800
Business: (201) 756-3836

Screening and Crisis
  Intervention Program
Zurbrugg Memorial Hospital
Riverside 08075
Director: Joan Mechlin
Emergency: (609) 764-1100
Business: (same)

New Mexico

* Suicide Prevention and Crisis
  Center of Albuquerque, Inc.
P.O. Box 4511
Albuquerque 87106
Director: Dorothy Trainor
Emergency: (505) 843-2941
Business: (same)

The Crisis Center
Box 3563
University Park Drive
Las Cruces 88001
Director: Byron King
Emergency: (505) 524-9241
Business: (505) 524-4081

The Bridge Crisis Intervention
  Center
113 Bridge Street
Las Vegas 87701
Director: Fran Clark
Emergency: (505) 425-6793
Business: (505) 425-5872

New York

Suicide Prevention Center
Kings County Hospital Center
606 Winthrop Street
Brooklyn 11203
Director: Dr. Eugene Becker
Emergency: (212) 462-3322
Business: (same)

Suicide Prevention and Crisis
  Service, Inc.
560 Main Street
Buffalo 14202
Director: Dr. Gene Brockopp
Emergency: (716) 854-1966
Business: (same)

Lifeline
Nassau County Medical Center
2201 Hempstead Turnpike
East Meadow 11554
Director: Michael King
Emergency: (516) 538-3111
Business: (516) 542-3446

* Suicide Prevention and Crisis
  Service
P.O. Box 312
Ithaca 14850
Director: Nina Miller
Emergency: (607) 272-1505
Business: (same)

Life Line-Health Association
  of Rochester and Monroe
  Counties, Inc.
973 East Avenue
Rochester 14607
Director:
  Betty G. Oppenheimer
Emergency: (716) 275-5151
Business: (same)

The Norman Vincent Peale
  Telephone Center
3 West Twenty-Ninth Street,
  10th Floor
New York 10001
Director: Rev. H. Leslie
  Christie
Emergency: (212) 686-3061
Business: (212) 686-3519

* National Save-a-Life League,
  Inc.
815 Second Avenue, Suite 409
New York 10017
Director: Harry M. Warren, Jr.
Emergency: (212) 736-6191
Business: (same)

Niagara County Crisis Center
527 Buffalo Avenue
Niagara Falls 14302
Director: Rev. Daniel Clark
Emergency: (716) 285-3515
Business: (716) 285-9636

24-Hour Mental Health
   Information and Crisis
   Phone Service
260 Crittenden Boulevard
Rochester 14620
Director: Dr. Haroutun
   Babigian
Emergency: (716) 275-4445
Business: (716) 275-4853

Suicide Prevention Service
29 Sterling Avenue
White Plains 10606
Director: Elaine S. Feiden
Emergency: (914) 949-0121
Business: (914) 949-6741

North Carolina

* Suicide and Crisis Service of
   Alamance County, Inc.
P.O. Box 2573
Burlington 27215
Director: C. Diane Jackson
Emergency: (919) 228-1720
Business: (same)

Crisis and Suicide Center
300 East Main Street
Durham 27701
Director: Mrs. Cobb W. Fox
Emergency: (919) 688-5504
Business: (919) 688-4363

Crisis Help and Suicide
   Prevention Service of Gaston
   County
508 West Main Avenue
Gastonia 28052
Director: Yvonne Spencer
Emergency: (704) 867-6373
Business: (704) 867-8971

Switchboard Crisis Center of
   Greensboro Drug Action
   Council
518 Summit Avenue
Greensboro 27405
Director: Bo Paul Kittrell
Emergency: (919) 275-9977
Business: (same)

Care
215 Mill Avenue
Jacksonville 28542
Directors: Artis G. Wood
                 Paul Bradford
Emergency: (919) 346-6292
Business: (919) 347-5118

Suicide and Crisis Intervention
   Service
Halifax County Mental Health
P.O. Box 577
Roanoake Rapids 27870
Director: Soong H. Lee
Emergency: (919) 537-2909
Business: (919) 537-6174

Crisis and Suicide Intervention
P.O. Box Q
Sanford 27330
Director: James Hampton
Emergency: (919) 776-5431
Business: (919) 775-4129

North Dakota

Suicide Prevention and
    Emergency Service
Ninth and Thayer
Bismarck 58501
Director: Dr. James O'Toole
Emergency: (701) 255-4124
Business: (same)

Suicide Prevention and Mental
    Health Center
700 First Avenue, South
Fargo 58102
Director: Dr. Eric Noble
Emergency: (701) 232-4357
Business: (701) 237-4513

Northeast Region Mental
    Health and Retardation
    Center
509 South Third Street
Grand Forks 58201
Director: Dr. James Hoyme
Emergency: (701) 772-7258
Business: (same)

St. Joseph's Hospital Suicide
    Prevention Center
St. Joseph's Hospital
Minot 58701
Supervisor: Sister Noemi
Emergency: (701) 838-5555
Business: (same)

Ohio

Support, Inc.
1361 West Market Street
Akron 44313
Director: Norma Rios
Emergency: (216) 864-7743
Business: (same)

Suicide Control Center
Ashtabula General Hospital
505 West Forty-Sixth Street
Ashtabula 44004
Director: Dr. F. Fournier
Emergency: (216) 993-6111
Business: (216) 998-4210

Crisis Intervention/Suicide
    Prevention
Athens Mental Health Center
Athens 45701
Director: Dr. David Caul
Emergency: (614) 592-3917
Business: (same)

Crisis Intervention Center
1341 Market Avenue, North
Canton 45701
Director: Dr. Herbert Heine
Emergency: (216) 452-9811
Business: (216) 452-6000

Crisis Center Scioto-Paint
    Valley Mental Health Center
425 Chestnut Street
Chillicothe 45601
Director: James R. Hagen,
    Ph.D.
Emergency: (614) 773-0760
Business: (same)

Psychiatric Emergency
    Evaluation and Referral
    Service
10900 Carnegie Avenue,
    Room 400
Cleveland 44106
Director: Everett C. Poe
Emergency: (216) 229-4547
Business: (same)

Suicide Prevention Service
1515 East Broad Street
Columbus 43205
Director: Cynthia Schuler-Hicks
Emergency: (614) 252-0354
Business: (same)

Suicide Prevention Center
184 Salem Avenue
Dayton 45406
Director: Nancy M. Yelton
Emergency: (513) 225-3093
Business: (same)

Town Hall II—Helpline
225 East College Street
Kent 44240
Director: Richard Fennig
Emergency: (216) 672-4357
Business: (216) 673-4560

Rescue, Inc.
One Stranahan Square
Toledo 43624
Director: Mrs. William Hook
Emergency: (419) 243-4251
Business: (same)

Crisis Hotline
2845 Bell Street
Zanesville 43701
Director: Dr. Robert Birch
Emergency: (614) 452-8403
Business: (614) 452-9121

Oregon

Crisis Service
127 N.A. Sixth Street
Corvallis 97330
Chairman: Mrs. Luke Krygier
Emergency: (503) 752-7030
Business: (503) 752-5107

Crisis Center
University of Oregon
Eugene 97403
Director: Howard van Arsdale
Emergency: (503) 686-4488
Business: (same)

Pennsylvania

Lifeline
520 East Broad Street
Bethlehem 18018
Chairman: Dr. A. A. Welsh
Emergency: (215) 691-0660
Business: (215) 867-8671

Suicide Prevention Center
Room 430, City Hall Annex
Philadelphia 19107
Director: Rose Marie Phillips
Emergency: (215) 686-4420
Business: (215) 686-4426

South Carolina

Crisis Intervention Service
Greenville Area Mental Health
715 Grove Road
Greenville 29605
Director: Rowland Hyde
Emergency: (803) 239-1021
Business: (803) 239-1011

Tennessee

Crisis Intervention Service
Helen Ross McNabb Center
1520 Cherokee Trail
Knoxville 37920
Director: Dr. Ken Carpenter
Emergency: (615) 637-9711
Business: (same)

* Suicide and Crisis
Intervention Service
P.O. Box 4068
Memphis 38104
Director: Mary Puckett
Emergency: (901) 726-5534
Business: (same)

* Crisis Intervention Center
250 Venture Circle
Nashville 37228
Director: Pat Higginbotham
Emergency: (615) 254-5505
Business: (same)

Texas

Call for Help
P.O. Box 60
Abilene 79604
Director: Nancy Hutchinson
Emergency: (915) 673-8211
Business: (same)

Suicide Prevention/Crisis
Service
Box 3044
Amarillo 79106
Director: Mrs. B. H. Rigler
Emergency: (806) 376-4251
Business: (806) 376-4431

Contact—Tarrant County
Box 6212
Arlington 76011
Director: Mary T. Murray
Emergency: (817) 277-2233
Business: (unlisted)

Information and Crisis Center
2434 Guadalupe
Austin 78705
Director: Ed Peters
Emergency: (512) 472-2411
Business: (512) 478-5695

Telephone Counseling and
Referral Service
c/o Counseling Center
The University of Texas
P.O. Box 8119
Austin 78712
Director: Dr. Ira Iscoe
Emergency: (512) 476-7073
Business: (512) 471-3515

Suicide Rescue, Inc.
5530 Bellaire Lane
Beaumont 77706
Director: James B. Hutto
Emergency: (713) 833-2311
Business: (same)

Suicide Prevention/Crisis
.Intervention
418 West Coolidge
Borger 79000
Director: Velma Boyd
Emergency: (806) 274-5389
Business: (806) 274-5331

* Crisis Intervention Service
P.O. Box 3075
Corpus Christi 78404
Director: Chesley L. Redus
Emergency: (512) 883-0271
Business: (same)

Suicide Prevention of Dallas,
Inc.
P.O. Box 19651
Dallas 75219
Director: James Hengstenberg
Emergency: (214) 521-9111
Business: (unlisted)

Denton Area Crisis Center
Flow Memorial Hospital
1310 Scripture Drive, Room 243
Denton 76201
Director: Dr. Norma Gilbert
Emergency: (817) 387-HELP
Business: (817) 382-1612

Help Line
P.O. Drawer 1108
Edinburgh 78539
Director: Bryan Robertson
Emergency: (512) 383-5341
Business: (512) 383-0121

Crisis Intervention
730 East Yandell
El Paso 79902
Director: Gill Lucker
Emergency: (915) 779-1800
Business: (915) 532-1481

Crisis Intervention Hotline
212 Burnett
Fort Worth 76102
Director: John Choate
Emergency: (817) 336-3355
Business: (817) 336-5921

Crisis Hotline
P.O. Box 4123
Houston 77014
Director: Hank Renteria
Emergency: (713) 527-9864
Business: (same)

Contact Lubbock, Inc.
P.O. Box 3334
Lubbock 79410
Director: Betty Ross
Emergency: (806) 765-8393
Business: (806) 765-7272

Suicide Rescue, Inc.
812 West Orange
Orange 77630
Director: Phyllis Smith
Emergency: (713) 883-5521
Business: (same)

Crisis Center
709 Cliffside
Richardson 75080
Director: Nancy Novak
Emergency: (214) 783-0008
Business: (same)

Crisis Center
P.O. Box 28061
San Antonio 78228
Director: Dr. Lawrence
    Schoenfeld
Emergency: (512) 732-2141
Business: (512) 732-9172

Crisis Helpline
Box 57545
Webster 77598
Director: Katrina Packard
Emergency: (713) 488-7222
Business: (713) 488-3528

Concern
P.O. Box 1945
Wichita Falls 76301
Director: Lucille Myers
Emergency: (817) 723-8231
Business: (same)

Utah

Crisis Intervention Service
156 Westminster Avenue
Salt Lake City 84115
Director: Dr. Norman
    Anderson
Emergency: (801) 484-8761
Business: (same)

Virginia

Northern Virginia Hotline
P.O. Box 187
Arlington 22210
Director: B. Kuehn
Emergency: (703) 522-4460
Business: (same)

* Suicide-Crisis Center, Inc.
3636 High Street
Portsmouth 23707
Director: Nancy Mills
Emergency: (804) 399-6395
Business: (same)

Washington

Crisis Clinic
3423 Sixth Street
Bremerton 98310
Director: Roger Gray
Emergency: (206) 373-2402
Business: (206) 373-7724

Emotional Crisis Service
1801 East Fourth
Olympia 98501
Director: Maxine Knutzen
Emergency: (206) 357-3681
Business: (206) 943-4760

* Crisis Clinic
1530 Eastlake East
Seattle 98102
Director: William E. Hershey
Emergency: (206) 329-1882
Business: (same)

Crisis Service
107 Division Street
Spokane 99202
Director: Dr. Z. Nelson
Emergency: (509) 838-4428
Business: (509) 838-4651

West Virginia

Suicide Prevention Service
418 Morrison Building
815 Quarrier Street
Charleston 25301
Director: Ted Johnson
Emergency: (304) 346-3332
Business: (304) 346-0424

Contact Huntington
520 Eleventh Street
Huntington 25705
Director: Rev. William Miller
Emergency: (304) 523-3448
Business: (304) 523-3440

Wisconsin

Eau Claire Suicide Prevention
   Center
1221 Whipple Street
Eau Claire 54701
Director: Barbara Larson
Emergency: (715) 834-6040
Business: (same)

Walworth County Mental
   Health Center
P.O. Box 290
Elkhorn 53121
Director: Richard Jones
Emergency: (414) 245-5011
Business: (414) 723-5400

* Emergency Services Dane
   County Mental Health
   Center
31 South Henry Street
Madison 53703
Director: Bernard Cesnik
Emergency: (608) 251-2341
Business: (same)

Psychiatric Emergency Services
8700 West Wisconsin Avenue
Milwaukee 53226
Director: Dr. George Currier
Emergency: (414) 258-2040
Business: (same)

Wyoming

Help Line, Inc.
Cheyenne 82001
Director: Carla Romano
Emergency: (307) 634-4469
Business: (same)